"How about hiring a temporary nanny?"

"A stranger?" He shook his head. "I don't think that's a good idea."

Maggie cleared her throat. "Not a stranger… But what about me? I could help with the boys when you're on duty."

"Oh, Maggie." His mother clapped her hands together. "How sweet of you to offer. That sounds like exactly what we need."

Maggie's gaze caught his. And he didn't like how her eyes made his heart accelerate.

"Unless, of course—" Maggie's lips thinned "—you have a personal objection to me caring for the boys."

Far from it. The opposite of objection, actually. That was what made him wary and hesitant.

He blew out a breath. "Thank you, Maggie. I hate to impose on you—"

"You're not imposing."

He pinched the bridge of his nose. "If you're sure you want to do this—"

"I'm sure." She gave him a tremulous smile. A smile that caused his heart to slam against his breastbone. "Do we have a deal?"

Lisa Carter and her family make their home in North Carolina. In addition to her Love Inspired novels, she writes romantic suspense for Abingdon Press. When she isn't writing, Lisa enjoys traveling to romantic locales, teaching writing workshops and researching her next exotic adventure. She has strong opinions on barbecue and ACC basketball. She loves to hear from readers. Connect with Lisa at lisacarterauthor.com.

Books by Lisa Carter

Love Inspired

Coast Guard Courtship
Coast Guard Sweetheart
Falling for the Single Dad
The Deputy's Perfect Match
The Bachelor's Unexpected Family
The Christmas Baby
Hometown Reunion
His Secret Daughter
The Twin Bargain
Stranded for the Holidays
A Mother's Homecoming

Visit the Author Profile page at Harlequin.com.

A Mother's Homecoming

Lisa Carter

LOVE INSPIRED
INSPIRATIONAL ROMANCE

LOVE INSPIRED®
INSPIRATIONAL ROMANCE

Recycling programs
for this product may
not exist in your area.

ISBN-13: 978-1-335-48821-3

A Mother's Homecoming

Copyright © 2020 by Lisa Carter

This is a work of fiction. Names, characters, places and incidents are either the
product of the author's imagination or are used fictitiously. Any resemblance
to actual persons, living or dead, businesses, companies, events or locales is
entirely coincidental.

This edition published by arrangement with Harlequin Books S.A.

For questions and comments about the quality of this book,
please contact us at CustomerService@Harlequin.com.

Love Inspired
22 Adelaide St. West, 40th Floor
Toronto, Ontario M5H 4E3, Canada
www.Harlequin.com

Printed in U.S.A.

And I will restore to you the years
that the locust hath eaten, the cankerworm,
and the caterpiller, and the palmerworm,
my great army which I sent among you.
—*Joel* 2:25

This book is dedicated to my husband,
in gratitude for new beginnings.

Chapter One

Maggie Arledge made it a point to never attend church on the second Sunday in May.

Yet here she stood on the sidewalk outside Truelove Community Church.

She'd spent the last three years trying to forget what had happened to her. And she'd been largely successful. Wrapping herself in a cocoon of numbness. Taking each day as it came. Staying too busy to dwell on the past.

Calling out greetings, friends surged around her. Like the river diverting around the boulder in its path before the water merged once more.

Her own personal boulder hadn't proved as easily overcome. Life and love flowed around her. Leaving her feeling high and dry. Unable to find a way to rejoin the flow.

Last year, she'd made a lame excuse for missing church. But this year she traded toddler duty with her friend AnnaBeth before realizing she'd signed up for the second Sunday in May.

Normally, she loved working in the toddler room. But today was fraught with reminders of what she'd lost. Compounding the loss, after church she and her dad would go to the cemetery to put flowers on her mother's grave.

During her childhood, she and her mom often had to attend church without her father. In a small-town police department, there was usually an emergency demanding the police chief's attention. He used to joke that crime didn't observe the Sabbath.

On the steps in front of the sanctuary, she spotted her dad talking to a tall, broad-shouldered man in a police uniform. *He must be the town's new police chief.*

With the opening of the town's new community center and her teaching schedule, she'd been too busy to pay much attention to the man hired to take her retiring father's position.

Early thirties, she estimated. Three or four years older than her. He had short-cropped black hair. Beard stubble shadowed a strong jawline.

Waving, her dad beckoned her over. "Magpie, come meet Bridger, our new chief."

The police chief's head snapped around. She walked toward them. Smile lines crinkled out from the corners of his startlingly blue eyes.

"Miss Arledge," he rasped in a gravelly voice.

And inside her chest, something altogether surprising fluttered like the barest flicker of a butterfly's wings.

She slammed to a standstill. "I—I'm late for the nursery. Sorry." Abruptly turning on her heel, she called over her shoulder, "N-nice to meet you."

In her haste to be away, she raced into the building. What was it about him that had affected her so? When he'd glanced at her, the sensation she felt sent her into flight. Somehow threatening the carefully protective barriers she'd placed around herself.

She didn't believe in love at first sight. Nor instant like, either. But she couldn't deny the awareness—a kind of recognition—that pulsed between them.

Inside the doors, she stopped to catch her breath. Recalling her inglorious dash, she cringed. The new police chief probably thought her the rudest, strangest person he'd ever not quite met.

But she *had* needed to go inside. The other worker was probably up to her eyeballs in toddlers.

A woman wearing a red rose in remembrance of a living mother bustled past Maggie, urging her brood toward the elementary classrooms.

Her stomach knotted again. During the unsettling encounter with the new police chief, she'd somehow managed to shove the significance of the day to the back of her mind.

Since moving home, she'd reconnected with her childhood faith. Become a regular attendee. Just not on the second Sunday of May—Mother's Day.

"You can do this," she whispered.

She pushed off toward the toddler room. If she could get through today, she'd be home free for another eleven months.

Keep moving forward.

Her motto for the last three years. Not fixating on the event that changed her life forever. Not wallowing in the wrenching loss that changed her heart forever.

She rushed down the hallway. Disengaging the child lock on the half door, she slipped into the toy-strewn classroom.

A small girl concentrated on building a tower of

blocks. A little boy pounded on the play workbench. She was thrilled to realize that the other worker was her close friend Callie.

Maggie stowed her purse in the cabinet underneath the sink. "Sorry I'm late."

The very pregnant Callie McAbee smiled. "Just in time."

With four-year-old Maisie, her husband's child from his first marriage, this baby would make a sweet addition to their family.

Callie was a dear friend. Yet sometimes her radiant happiness scraped still-raw places in Maggie's heart. Reminding her of all she'd never have.

Inexplicably, her thoughts flitted to the new police chief.

Callie nudged her chin toward the open door. "I think our numbers are about to double."

Holding tightly to the hands of two toddler twin boys, an older woman hesitated on the threshold.

Maggie's heart skipped a beat. But she pushed forward. "I'm Maggie Arledge." She ushered them inside. "I don't think we've met."

Not identical, the twins did share the same big brown eyes. So, so adorable in their pint-size khakis and blue button-down shirts.

"I'm Wilda. We're new in town and decided to visit GeorgeAnne's church today." The sixtysomething woman with kind blue eyes brought the two boys forward. "My grandsons are almost two. Are we in the right place?"

"GeorgeAnne is my aunt." She reached to take the navy blue backpack from the woman with the salt-and-pepper hair. "And you are most definitely in the right place."

Letting go of one boy's pudgy little hand, Wilda eased the backpack off her shoulder. She handed it to her. "You must be Tom Arledge's daughter."

Clinging to his grandmother's side, the darker-haired twin peered uncertainly at Maggie.

She deposited the backpack into an empty cubby. "You know my dad, too?"

"My son is Truelove's new chief of police. He had to finish a case at the office so we're meeting him here."

As she clicked the half door shut, heat bloomed in her cheeks over her out-of-the-ordinary reaction to Wilda's obviously *married* son. "Weekend duty is tough."

The matronly woman shrugged. "We're a law enforcement family. Weekend duty comes with the territory."

Her father had been a good police chief. The citizens of Truelove knew he'd taken his duty to protect and serve seriously. Sometimes to his own family's detriment. He would be missed.

She handed Wilda the check-in paperwork to complete. "Hello, guys." Carefully tucking her skirt around her legs, she crouched to their height.

Letting go of the other child's hand, Wilda filled in the blanks on the paper. "Everyone in Truelove has been so friendly. Boys, introduce yourselves to Miss Maggie, please."

The twin with the short blond curls stuck his baby thumb into his chest. "Me Wostin."

Wilda's lips twitched. "This is Austin."

She turned to the other child, who had straight brown hair. "And what's your name, sweetheart?" Shy, he hid his face.

Austin flung out his arm. "He Wogan."

She arched her brow at Wilda.

Their grandmother smiled. "Logan."

She vaguely recalled hearing the new police chief was from Raleigh, the state capital. But why was his mother, and not his wife, dropping off their sons?

Aunt GeorgeAnne would probably have the scoop.

"Would you mind if I stayed with the boys this morning?" Wilda bit her lip. "With all the changes in their lives, they feel a bit uprooted. We're protective of them, you see."

Maggie didn't understand, but she didn't mind, either. "We'd love for you to stay."

Callie drifted over to introduce herself. "You may be put to work. Needing a village takes on new meaning in the toddler classroom."

The older woman laughed. "Land of lakes, I wouldn't have it any other way." She waved the clipboard. "Where do I put this?"

Callie deposited the paperwork in the tray on the counter for the church staff.

"GeorgeAnne has been so helpful." Wilda steered the twins toward the toys. "She's even introduced me to two members of the Double Name Club."

Maggie and Callie exchanged amused glances.

GeorgeAnne Allen. ErmaJean Hicks. IdaLee Moore. Better known as the Truelove Matchmakers, the elderly trifecta were notorious for taking their civic duty and the town slogan—Truelove, Where True Love Awaits— to heart.

Maybe because she'd always been a tomboy, Maggie had never been caught in their crosshairs. Which suited her just fine. Marriage and family would never happen for her.

And she'd done her best to reconcile herself to making the most of the life God had given her. Her second chance.

Spotting a plastic big rig truck, Austin fell to the braided rug. Logan squatted in front of a toy barnyard. Callie removed a large box of cheese crackers from an overhead cabinet.

Maggie's aunt GeorgeAnne poked her iron-gray cap of hair around the frame of the half door. "Hey!"

The three of them jerked.

Angular and somewhat bony, GeorgeAnne pushed the black-framed glasses higher on the bridge of her nose. "Did my niece tell you about the kid classes she teaches at the rec center, Wilda?"

"What kind of classes?"

Maggie sank to the carpet between the boys. "Good morning to you, too, Aunt G."

Typical GeorgeAnne. She blew in like a hurricane. No-nonsense and straight to the point.

Seventyish, GeorgeAnne flattened her thin lips into what, for her, constituted a smile. "The class is for little kids who like to jump and run and roll. Does that sound like something your boys like to do?"

Looking up, Austin nodded. "Me do." Logan kept his eyes glued to the small barn.

"I think your tumbling class sounds perfect." Wilda settled herself in the gliding rocker. "I love them dearly, but I don't mind telling you they can wear a body out."

"That's what Tumbling Tots does best." GeorgeAnne smirked. "Teaches a few basic skills. And tuckers them out two mornings a week."

"Fantastic." Wilda blew out a breath. "Where do I sign up?"

"We're starting a new session Monday morning. Class begins at nine." Sitting crisscross applesauce on the rug, Maggie handed Logan a toy sheep. Austin zoomed a plastic tractor around them. "Dress them in loose-fitting, comfortable play clothes, and they'll be good to go." She resisted the impulse to touch their silken baby hair.

Wilda smiled. "Isn't it just like God to allow our paths to cross? Right when we need it most?"

The morning flew by. She so enjoyed getting to know Austin, Logan and their grandmother. After the service, parents started coming in to collect their children. Wilda and the twins were the last to say goodbye. Emotion clogged Maggie's throat.

Mustn't cry. She dug her nails into her palms. *Not now. Not ever.*

After setting the room to rights, she and Callie left at the same time. Callie, on the arm of her wonderful husband, Jake. Treacherous tears once again stung her eyelids.

Stop with the self-pity, Mags.

Outside, her father waited for her under the shade of a towering oak. She sighed. He was probably annoyed by her strange behavior earlier.

"I'm sorry, Dad."

"No need to be sorry, Magpie." He ducked his head. "I miss your mother, too," he whispered.

Maggie was taken aback to see moisture dotting his dark eyes.

She missed her mother more than she could say, but today it wasn't her mother she missed the most. Though if her mother had been alive three years ago, maybe she would have made different choices.

That night in Atlanta, she could've so easily died. God had spared her life. And she didn't mean to waste it.

Yet in the wee hours of the night, when the sorrow was at its peak, she consoled herself with the knowledge she'd done the right thing. The unselfish thing.

Because that was what mothers did.

Her gaze was drawn to Wilda and the twins. Crossing the little footbridge spanning the creek, they headed toward the parking lot. The handsome new chief stood between his pickup truck and a black minivan.

Maggie sent a prayer of gratitude skyward for what she did have—her father, her home and a job she loved.

Plus she was excited at the possibility of getting to know Austin and Logan on Monday.

Her dad offered his arm. "Ready to head to the cemetery?"

Eyes flicking toward the minivan and the pickup pulling out onto the highway, she exhaled. The Father of good gifts had given her a special gift on this hardest of days. Wilda was right.

Just when she'd needed it most.

Early Monday morning, Bridger Hollingsworth parked the white SUV that came with the new job in the last available spot outside the Mason Jar Diner. The parking places out front and along the side of the town green were filled.

According to his predecessor, Tom Arledge, the Jar was a popular local hangout. Tom had invited him for a quick debrief before he headed to the police department down the block.

Overhead, a bell jangled as he entered the café. Bustling waitresses carried trays of food from the cutout window behind the counter to customers. As was his habit—a habit that had kept him alive thus far—he immediately scanned the occupants of the diner, scoping out potential risks.

With an accompanying hum of conversation, men and women of varying ages sat scattered around the café. A young guy in blue overalls from an automotive shop. At a far table underneath a bulletin board, a trio of elderly ladies. The town and its inhabitants were everything his research had led him to believe about Truelove.

Farmers. Ranchers. Local businessmen. A tight-knit, friendly community. Low crime rate. A good place to put down roots and raise his family.

The aroma of yeasty biscuits and fried potatoes wafted across his nostrils. His stomach growled. Maybe not such a bad idea to talk shop with Arledge and feed his belly at the same time.

Spotting him in the doorway, the lanky ex-lawman motioned him toward the section of booths. "Good to see you again, Hollingsworth."

He shook the older gentleman's hand. "Good to see you, too, sir." Taking off the regulation hat, he cut his eyes at the crowded diner. "Is it always this busy at the Mason Jar?"

"The usual breakfast crowd." Tom grinned. "Before we order, though, I want to introduce you to some of the fine citizens of Truelove."

Leaving his hat on the table, he followed Tom to a cluster of men seated on the counter stools. Bridger's late father had been a police chief in a Raleigh suburb. And although this was his first venture into an administrative position, he knew the drill.

As police chief, his job was threefold: to maintain

a good working relationship with the town council, to provide leadership to the officers he'd supervise and to bolster law enforcement's relationship with the community.

He appreciated Tom's efforts to help him become part of the community. A subtle stamp of approval. A passing of the torch. Bestowing the mantle of responsibility in the eyes of the Truelove public.

Amid jokes of being put out to pasture, Tom led him from table to table, greeting the townspeople and shaking hands.

Nash Jackson, an orchard grower. Dwight Fleming, owner of a white-water rafting company. The mayor's wife. A pastor.

The three elderly ladies belonged to something called the Double Name Club. Whatever that was. He flicked his eyes at Tom, who appeared to have stuck his tongue in his cheek.

But everyone was welcoming. The Double Name Club members were especially enthusiastic.

He was good with names and faces. He had to be. More than once, his life had depended on it.

Finishing the rounds, Tom slid into their booth. "How'd your first case go this weekend?"

A waitress left a carafe of coffee and two empty cups on the table.

"Patrol caught a couple of teenagers tagging the side of an old barn with spray paint. No big deal." He sank onto the vinyl seat across from Tom. "But paperwork is paperwork."

Tom poured the steaming coffee into the porcelain mugs. "Good ole American bureaucracy at its finest.

Not as exciting as those drug busts you used to work. I hope you won't get too bored in sleepy ole Truelove."

He wrapped his hand around the mug. "I'm hoping those adrenaline- and pulse-pumping days are behind me."

After the humiliation of what happened with his former fiancée, Chelsea, he was also done with betrayal and lies.

"I want you to know how much I appreciate everything you've done for me, Chief." Bridger cleared his throat. "This new position provides my family the opportunity for a new start."

Tom shook his head. "You're the chief now. And it was how you presented yourself during the interview with the town council that secured you this job, son. Not me."

He leaned forward. "I don't aim to let you—or the town—down, sir."

"Your dad and I went through the academy together. One of the best men I ever knew. A real straight arrow." Tom winked. "I have no doubt the apple doesn't fall far from the tree. You'll do fine, Bridger."

Venturing over, the waitress took their breakfast order.

"Unless there's a major incident, you'll keep regular office hours." While they ate, Tom passed along a few tips for surviving and thriving in Truelove. "You can leave the weekend duty to the less senior officers. But, of course, a police chief is always on call if needed."

He pushed away his now-empty plate. "I'm hoping to have more time with the boys. To build a solid relationship with them."

Tom laid down his fork. "How long have you been their guardian?"

A sharp pinch of grief assailed him. "Since my brother and his wife died four months ago. I never expected to be their guardian. With Mom getting on in years and my sister expecting her third child, everyone agreed it was best." He sighed. "I never reckoned on marriage or a family of my own, though."

Tom's brows bunched. "Why's that?"

His shoulders rose and fell. "Relationships are hard enough. With the unique hazards in our line of work, relationships have proved impossible for me. Or, at least, healthy relationships."

Tom gazed at him over the rim of his mug. "Sounds like there's a story there."

"Not a pleasant one." His lips twisted. "Experience can be a bitter teacher."

"You probably just haven't found the right woman yet. And even then, it takes work, for sure. It's not easy, but no matter the job, nothing worthwhile ever is. Marriage and family are some of life's greatest joys."

He kept further opinions on the matter to himself. His former, uncertain lifestyle hadn't lent itself to developing viable relationships. For the foreseeable future, casual dating was out for him, too.

Bridger had no intention of allowing the twins to get attached to a woman, only to lose her when the relationship inevitably turned sour. They'd already suffered far too much loss in their young lives.

He could no longer be away for weeks on end as an undercover cop. Once he assumed guardianship, he'd been determined to do everything in his power to minimize the risks his chosen profession imposed. After losing their parents so unexpectedly, Austin and Logan needed stability and love.

Bringing him to Truelove. A chance for him and the boys to make a good life together. Even if it meant major life changes and moving halfway across the state. Yet without his mother's willingness to relocate and look after the twins when he was on duty, he could've never made the move.

Silver-haired Tom eased out of the booth. "I'd best be off. Don't want to make you late." He snagged the bill off the table.

"Wait, sir. Let me—"

"Next time, it's on you." Tom clapped a hand on his shoulder. "Welcome to Truelove, Chief Hollingsworth. It's your town now, but I'm here if you ever find yourself needing an old man's advice."

Bridger lingered for a few moments. Sipping his coffee, he enjoyed the view out the plate glass window overlooking Main Street.

On the horizon, wave upon wave of undulating blue-green ridges enfolded the charming town like the worn but comforting arms of a beloved grandmother. The Appalachians were old mountains. The mountains defined the citizens of Truelove. As did the gushing river, forming a horseshoe around the town limits.

A slower pace of life. The simplicity and goodness of small things. Parenting the twins and becoming police chief were a responsibility and privilege he didn't take lightly.

"I'm glad I caught you." An attractive young woman in sneakers, black capri leggings and a bright pink workout top threw herself into the seat across from him. "We didn't get a chance to talk before you left this morning."

Startled, he jolted. Coffee dribbled down the sides of the mug in his hand.

"Oh!" Her large dark brown eyes widened. "You're not—I saw the sleeve of your uniform and thought—" She blushed. "I keep forgetting Dad's gone civilian."

His insides did a nosedive. *Her*. It was her.

When her gaze had caught his yesterday on the sidewalk at church, his heart had sped up. Which made no sense. Completely irrational. And yet...

"You're Maggie Arledge?"

She nodded, setting her dark brown ponytail in motion. "Sorry about that." She gestured toward the puddle of coffee.

"No problem."

Their brief encounter yesterday had disconcerted him. To a guy like him, who prized order and reason above all else, it was disturbing. He'd done his best to put her out of his mind. A semisuccessful effort. Until now...

"I—I just didn't hear you coming." He raked his hand over his head. "I usually don't have my back to the door."

"But let me guess." Yanking several napkins from the canister, she mopped the table. "Dad automatically took this seat first."

"Old habits die hard."

"I'm also sorry about rushing away yesterday." Flushing, she bit her lip. "It's nice to officially meet you, Chief Bridger."

She took a big breath as if gathering her courage. Extending her hand across the table, she gave him a tremulous smile. And in that split second, she went from attractive to very pretty.

When his hand closed over hers, a bolt of electricity shot up his elbow. Blinking, she drew back.

She'd felt that, too. Static electricity maybe?

He dropped his hand into his lap. "Just Bridger." He rubbed his hand against his uniform slacks. "It's nice to officially meet you, too, Maggie."

Uncertainty flickered across her face. "I—I should go." She propelled herself out of the booth.

What was it with the sudden exits?

Grabbing his hat, he scrambled out after her. "Wait."

Poised beside the booth to flee, she stood about five foot six to his six-foot height.

He strangled the brim of his hat. "Um…" He reddened.

Athletic and fit, she looked at him, eyebrow raised.

Yet other than the irrational impulse to halt her precipitous leave-taking, he didn't know what to say. It wasn't like him to get flustered over a woman. Undercover work required a cool head and, oftentimes, a glib tongue.

She inclined her head, sending her ponytail waving. "Yes, Mr. Bridger?"

He frowned. Was there an unspoken mountain rule about the casual use of given names?

"It's Bridger," he grunted.

She moistened her lips. "Bridger…"

Feeling a small stab of triumph, he loosened his tongue. "I expect we'll run into each other again."

She gave him a curious look. "Truelove is a small town. Can't help but run into everybody on a regular basis."

"We're also going to be neighbors." He fingered his hat. "I bought the farm next to your dad's."

She touched her hand to her throat. "I—I didn't know you were the one who bought the old Lassiter place. It's a lovely property."

Not near as lovely as the woman standing before him.

Over Sunday lunch, his mother had talked about the people she'd met at church, including the fitness instructor. "The boys are looking forward to taking your class this morning."

Her face transformed. "They're so sweet. Speaking of class, I'd best head to the rec center."

Bridger walked her out of the diner. And despite what he'd said to her father, suddenly he couldn't help hoping the twins weren't the only Hollingsworths who'd get the chance to know Maggie Arledge better.

Chapter Two

Driving to the recreation center, Maggie couldn't get over her reaction to the ruggedly handsome Chief Bridger. Other than her dad, most men made her anxious. And if they got too close, sometimes it triggered a panic attack. Expecting the same, she'd worked herself up to do the polite thing and shake his hand.

To her amazement, the touch of his hand had sparked an unfamiliar but not unpleasant sensation.

After what had happened to her in Atlanta, she feared she'd never experience feelings of attraction ever again. At the touch of his hand, a reassuringly normal tingle sent goose bumps skittering across her skin.

Except… She met his sons at church yesterday. Was he married? There'd been no wedding ring on his finger.

Okay… So she'd looked.

But what did she know? Some men didn't wear a wedding band. Yet there'd been no mention of a wife, either. Perhaps he was divorced and had custody of his children.

Mind your own business.

On the outskirts of town, her vehicle clattered over

the bridge spanning the rushing river below. It had been a snowy winter, resulting in a heavy spring runoff.

Passing the welcome-to-Truelove sign, she averted her gaze. Not that she needed to look to know what it said. Like every other Truelove resident, the motto had been emblazoned into her brain practically from birth.

Truelove, North Carolina—Where True Love Awaits.

Just not for her. But suddenly Chief Bridger's chiseled features flashed through her mind. And that slow, easy smile of his. A pulse-thumping, ridiculously stomach-quivering smile.

What is your deal, Mags? Enough already.

Blowing out pent-up oxygen, she turned into the parking lot of the state-of-the-art recreational facility. Over the last two years, she'd worked closely with county officials to make the center a reality. Gathering her gym bag, she sprinted into the building.

Great-Aunt GeorgeAnne stood behind the information counter in the atrium. "Slow down, Mary Margaret."

Only her aunt, the de facto leader of the Double Name Club, ever called Maggie by her full name.

"Can't." She panted. "I'm late."

"None of your students have arrived. Plenty of time to catch your breath."

She slowed, but didn't stop.

Her aunt was one of a dozen volunteers who worked the desk during the week. Which in actuality meant GeorgeAnne supervised the rotation of volunteers. And she ran the center like a well-oiled machine. Not unlike how she'd run the local hardware store before her retirement.

"Got to set out the mats," Maggie called over her shoulder.

"Already done."

Grinding to a halt, she returned to the information desk. "You didn't have to do that, but thanks, Aunt G."

Her aunt peered over the rim of her glasses. "As I was leaving the Jar, I saw you talking to Wilda's son. I thought you might be delayed."

She reddened. Where there was one Truelove matchmaker, the other two couldn't be too far away. She hadn't seen them, but apparently they'd seen her.

Having supposedly handed over the reins of the hardware business to her sons, GeorgeAnne wasn't one to remain idle—hence the meddlesome matchmaking.

GeorgeAnne leaned her elbows on the counter. "Since you're dying to know, I'll go ahead and tell you."

"I'm not d—"

"He's single."

Maggie suspected her beleaguered cousins had donated a sizable contribution to the rec center on the condition the director offer their forthright matriarch a temporary job. Anything to keep her out of their hair.

GeorgeAnne tilted her head, giving Maggie the once-over. "I do wish you'd at least put on some lipstick this morning." She tsked. "A little paint never did an old barn any harm."

Maggie fought the urge to roll her eyes.

With GeorgeAnne's blunt-cut hair and total lack of regard for makeup of any variety, that was rich coming from her aunt.

"You of all people know I'm not looking for..." She flung out her hand. "For..."

"For love?" GeorgeAnne's steel blue eyes gentled. "A life lived without love is no life at all."

She swallowed. "You know why that life is impossible for me, Aunt G."

Her aunt pursed her lips. "Nothing is impossible. Not when it comes to love."

Only GeorgeAnne knew what had happened to her in Atlanta. And Maggie never wanted anyone else to ever learn the truth about what she'd been through.

Though a more unlikely confidante she could hardly imagine than her pull-no-punches, unsentimental great-aunt.

But two years ago, within a few days of returning home, GeorgeAnne had seen something amiss. And Maggie found herself telling her aunt about the attack and its aftermath.

The front doors whooshed open and shut. A welcome distraction from painful thoughts. The art instructor waved, but headed toward the art studio at the back of the building.

Once the teacher was out of earshot, GeorgeAnne laid her hands flat on top of the counter. "The new police chief is a good-looking man."

The new police chief was an *exceptionally* handsome man. But she knew better than to let that slip. Any hint of romantic interest, and her matchmaker aunt would be like white on rice at the possibilities.

"You know I don't do girlie-girl, G. I take after you." She kissed her aunt's wrinkly cheek to soften her words. "Strong. Capable. Nobody's victim."

GeorgeAnne sighed. "You can be athletic and girlie at the same time. And it is in love we find our greatest strength."

She strangled the strap of her gym bag. "I'm not ready." She doubted she'd ever be ready, or brave enough, for a relationship.

Yet once, like most young girls, she'd dreamed of fairy-tale romance. It was just that sometimes—like when meeting the new police chief—her heart forgot what her head already knew.

Those dreams were lost to her now.

A parent and one of her students walked into the atrium. She used their entrance to make her escape. Right off the lobby, she taught her classes in the center's smaller gym.

The other Tumbling Tots soon followed, including Wilda and the twins. It was a small group, designed for more one-on-one instruction and parent-child interaction.

She didn't have time to do more than glance at the children's first names on the attendance sheet.

Holding on to the twins' hands and gazing at the obstacle course, Wilda appeared flustered.

"Don't worry, Miss Wilda. I can help one of the twins move through the stations."

"That would be great." Letting go of Logan, Wilda smoothed a hand over her hair. "I didn't get here in time to fill out the registration, but GeorgeAnne told us to head straight inside so we didn't miss anything. I always forget what a production it is to get these guys out the door each morning."

Maggie crouched in front of the boys. "Would one of you help me show the other kids how each station works?"

Dark-haired Logan held back, but with a sunny, never-met-a-stranger smile, Austin took hold of her hand. "Me do, Magwee."

When his little hand folded around her fingers, her heart experienced a frisson of both joy and pain.

Getting to her feet, she addressed the mothers. "I have information packets for each parent." She gestured toward the cubby unit where the children and parents left their shoes. "There's also a week-by-week listing of the social and spatial skills we'll cover during the spring session."

She explained a few safety rules about parents spotting their child as they made their way through the circuit.

"But I've talked long enough." She smiled at the boys and girls standing with their moms in a semicircle. "Let the fun begin. Follow me," she beckoned.

Utilizing Austin as a living, breathing visual aid, she took the class through the course laid out around the mats on the floor.

With low, happy music playing, she helped Austin pick his way along the crayon-bright, foam balance beam. The crawl-through tunnel was next. She steadied him as he climbed up the soft wedge incline and down again.

Together they navigated the agility cones. At the final station, she demonstrated how to leapfrog from one foam lily pad to the next. It didn't take him long to catch on.

She monitored the progress of each child. Several kids had been enrolled in the winter tumbling session. She wanted to make sure everyone was having fun and a successful, confidence-building playtime. The thirty-minute class flew by.

To close out the first class, she gathered the children and their moms into a huge circle. Everyone took hold of the giant colorful parachute. Billowing the silken chute, they sang a goodbye song, and she dismissed them to put on their shoes.

"See you on Wednesday."

Many of the children hugged her before heading out with their moms. Their exuberance and wide-eyed wonder at the joys of life warmed her heart every time. Of all the fitness classes she taught at the center, the Tumbling Tots class was her favorite.

"That *was* fun." Wilda wrestled Logan's foot into his small sneaker. "You're good with children, Maggie."

She tried to help the very independent Austin put on his socks. "Sometimes I think I ought to be the one paying the rec center for allowing me to do something I love so much."

"Your passion in teaching them how to stay fit and strong shines through."

Maggie blew a strand of hair that had escaped from her ponytail. "I'm guessing twins provide a built-in workout."

Wilda laughed. "Which is why parenting is better suited for someone your age."

Maggie didn't answer. Wilda had no way of knowing how her words struck a nerve. The affectionate hugs of her students were the closest she'd ever come to satisfying the yearning of her empty arms. A temporary measure to lessen the longing to hold her own children.

Setting Austin on his feet, she helped Wilda get off the floor.

"With the weather warming, next time I'll know to dress them in sandals." Wilda planted her hands on her hips. "We'd best head out. The twins' second birthday is next month. We're going to the mall in Asheville this afternoon to get a head start on my shopping."

"June is a wonderful birthday month." She laid her hand on Austin's blond curls. "You met Callie on Sunday. She rented out the Tumbling Tot gym for Maisie's gymnastic-theme party."

"Maybe next year." Wilda settled her purse strap over her arm. "I'm taking the boys to my daughter's house in Fayetteville so they can celebrate with their cousins." She took firm hold of each child's hand. "Boys, tell Miss Maggie goodbye."

Slipping free of his grandmother, Austin gave her an enthusiastic hug around her knees. "Bye-bye, Miss Magwee."

The more solemn twin, Logan, gave her a small wave.

Wiggling her fingers at him, she smiled. "See you later, alligator."

Austin laughed. "He not gator, Miss Magwee."

She pretended to be surprised. "He's not? Are you sure?" And was rewarded when Logan's mouth curved.

Her heart melted. Such sweet, good boys. Following them out to the lobby, she stood beside her aunt at the reception desk. She watched until Wilda drove away in the black minivan.

"I haven't seen you smile like that in a long time." GeorgeAnne patted her arm. "You look happy, Mary Margaret."

"I am happy." She was surprised to find it true.

"I like that family." GeorgeAnne tapped her finger to her chin. "What do you think?"

What she didn't like was the look in her aunt's eye. "I love the boys. Their grandmother, too."

"And what about our new police chief?"

Her aunt was definitely on a fishing expedition. Best to proceed with caution. "He seems efficient and thorough."

"A glowing review." GeorgeAnne rolled her eyes. "If you're in the market for a vacuum cleaner."

She sniffed. "I'm not interested in Chief Bridger, Aunt G."

The old lady lifted her chin. "I must say, you two looked right cozy at the diner this morning."

"Appearances can be deceiving." She gulped. A lesson she learned the hard way. "Now, if you'll excuse me, I need to get ready for another class."

But over the next few days, try as she might, she couldn't shake the memory of the new chief's smoldering blue gaze and her almost visceral response to him.

A week later, Bridger stood in the rec center lobby outside the small gym. Through the plate glass window, he watched the twins make their way around the obstacle course with the other children. He planned to surprise the boys—and give his mother a break—with lunch at the diner.

True to his buoyant nature, Austin tackled the equipment with the same gusto he applied to everything in his young life. His grandmother could barely keep pace as he flung himself without fear from one station to the next. A daredevil in the making. But a little fear was a healthy thing.

Interestingly, the slower-to-warm Logan had decided to make the lithesome Maggie Arledge his friend today. His approach to each challenge was thoughtful. Cautious. And he reached the finished line, too. Only less battered and bruised.

Coming around the counter, GeorgeAnne Allen thrust a brochure at him. "Here's the spring schedule of classes. The family membership plan will give you access to the pool." Her steely blue eyes scrutinized him. "And the weight room. I'm sure you'll want to set the example for the men in our town."

As a former undercover cop, he didn't intimidate easily. But frankly, the old lady terrified him. He had the feeling she was nobody's fool. He wouldn't want to find himself on the receiving end of her ire.

He had his own physical training routine, but community relations were part of his job.

"I'll definitely consider joining, Miss GeorgeAnne." His gaze strayed to the window where Maggie looped the children through a set of orange cones.

"You do that, Chief. Of course, my niece spends a great deal of time here at the rec center, too."

His eyes cut to the old woman.

Smirking, she cocked her head. "But you're a smart man. I'm sure you've already thought of that."

Maggie Arledge was definitely an incentive to get a gym membership. He ran his hand through his hair.

GeorgeAnne snorted. "I'll get the membership application for you." She moved away toward the desk.

He scanned the array of classes offered at the center. Maggie taught most of the fitness courses. A senior adult Silver Sneaker class. A Baby Mama workout for pregnant mothers. Gym classes for every age level of children. He didn't wonder at how she stayed so trim. Instead, he wondered if she ever stood still.

Observing her interaction with the kids, it was clear how much she enjoyed children. She was already bringing out the best in Austin and Logan. Laughing at Austin's antics, yet keeping him safe from foolhardy disaster. Encouraging Logan to tackle new adventures, yet providing comfort if at first he didn't succeed.

Bridger rubbed the back of his neck. He could learn a lot from Maggie's seemingly effortless connection with the twins. He hadn't managed to get Logan to open up to him.

Much of the time, he felt at a loss to provide what they needed. He thanked God for his mother's willingness to help him learn the parenting ropes.

He watched as Maggie pulled out a small-size parachute. Standing in a large circle, each child and parent grasped hold of an edge. She sang out the name of a kid, and everyone billowed the chute as the child ran under and then out again. After giving each toddler a turn, she ended the class.

Bridger stepped aside as parents and their children streamed out of the gym into the lobby. Accompanied by Maggie, his mother and the twins were the last to emerge.

"Son." His mother's face lifted. "What a nice surprise."

Maggie's dark eyes flicked to him and lit. Was he imagining the gleam was because of him? And why did he find himself hoping it was true?

His mother took his arm. "Maggie, let me introduce you to my son."

Bridger squared his shoulders. "We've already—"

"I met—" Maggie bit her lip.

Bridger fingered the brim of his hat. "We met the other day at the diner, Mom."

His mother's eyebrows rose. "I didn't realize you two knew each other."

Over at the desk, GeorgeAnne had gone silent. No

doubt straining to catch every word of their conversation. Tom had warned him the small town loved nothing more than gossip. And that instant messaging was nothing compared to the Truelove grapevine.

His mother patted Austin and Logan. "The boys love Maggie's class."

"I love having them in class." Maggie crouched to their height. "Can I get a goodbye hug from two of my favorite students?"

Immediately, Austin threw his arms around her, nearly knocking her off her feet. "Bye, Miss Magwee."

She rocked backward onto the heels of her sneakers. To steady her, Bridger put his hand on Maggie's shoulder. With a sharp intake of breath, she flinched.

Chagrined, he removed his hand. He hadn't meant to startle her. He didn't usually go around touching people.

Her gaze locked onto his. But it was the look in her eyes that stopped him cold. An emotion just this side of blind terror.

Bridger became transfixed by the pulsing vein in the hollow of her throat. Yet after a split second, her breathing evened and her shoulders relaxed. The moment passed. She threw him a slightly apologetic smile.

Logan squeezed her hand. "See you waiter, a-weegator."

The lost look in her eyes faded. She gave him a one-armed hug. "After a while, crocodile."

Bridger glanced between the child and Maggie. Was it only him that made her jumpy?

Logan tugged at Bridger's pant leg. "I wike a-weegators and cwoc-o-diles."

"Good to know." His lips twitched. "Thanks for the info, Logan."

It was the first time in four months Logan had initiated any sort of conversation with him. Maybe their teacher's influence could help bridge the gap in his relationship with the quieter twin.

Maggie got to her feet. "Sounds like a trip to the zoo might be in our police chief's future."

He chuckled. "But first, I came to take the boys and my mother out to lunch at the diner. Mom, what do you say?"

"I say yes to any meal I don't have to—" His mother's phone trilled within her purse.

Digging it out, she glanced at the screen. "It's your sister, Shannon." Hand over one ear, his mother answered the call. "Shan—oh, no."

He tensed. "Mom?"

GeorgeAnne came out from the desk. The twins wandered over to inspect the nearby mural.

His mother's face paled. "Thank you so much for letting me know," she said into the phone. "Let me talk to my son. I'll call you as soon as I can make arrangements." She clicked off.

Bridger took hold of her arm. "What's wrong, Mom?" His stomach knotted.

First Jeff and Dana. Had something happened to Shannon's husband, Paul, who was deployed to Afghanistan? Would the hits never stop coming? How much more could one family be expected to bear?

Widening his stance, he braced for another emotional blow. "Is it Paul?"

"As far as I know, Paul is well, but on an undisclosed mission. Shannon's neighbor called to tell me she's gone into premature labor."

Bridger winced. "She's only seven months along. Are she and the baby going to be all right?"

His mother tucked the cell into her purse. "Shannon's at the base hospital. The doctors are doing everything they can to stop the progression of labor."

Bridger resettled his hat on his head. "What about her other little ankle-biters?"

He adored his niece and nephew. With their mom whisked to the hospital, they must be so scared.

"Their neighbor is watching them for now, but..." His mother's gaze dropped.

GeorgeAnne frowned. "Even if the doctors stop the premature labor, she'll be in no shape to take care of two children."

His mother sighed. "Once she's released from the hospital, Shannon will probably have to be on bed rest for the remainder of her pregnancy."

GeorgeAnne nodded. "Putting off the delivery as long as possible. Giving the baby every chance to fully develop before birth."

"Shannon needs you, Mom."

"You and the twins need me, too."

He scrubbed his hand over his face. "In Raleigh, we would've only been an hour away from her."

"You sought the Lord about the decision to relocate. And He confirmed it in so many ways." His mother jutted her chin. "We've been thrown a curveball, but this is where the rubber meets the road. Time to put our trust where our faith lies."

After the fiasco with Chelsea and the death of his brother and sister-in-law, it had taken him a long time to find his way back to the spiritual foundation of his childhood. He'd struggled. But through the grace of

God, he'd come out on the other side a different and better man.

He exhaled. "You need to go take care of Shannon and the rug rats."

"But what about the boys?"

"We'll manage, Mom. I'm not sure how, but somehow we will."

GeorgeAnne tapped her foot on the linoleum. "How about hiring a temporary nanny?"

With the hypersensitivity he seemed to possess when it came to Maggie, he realized she'd gone stock-still.

"A stranger?" He shook his head. "I don't think that's a good idea, Miss GeorgeAnne."

Maggie cleared her throat. "Not a stranger... But what about me? I could help with the boys when you're on duty."

"Oh, Maggie." His mother clapped her hands together. "How sweet of you to offer."

He stiffened. "Maggie already has a job, Mom."

"I'm sure something could be arranged to accommodate both your schedules." GeorgeAnne folded her arms over her plaid cotton shirt. "Maggie teaches a few classes at the rec center, but not every day, nor all day. She could bring the boys with her on the days she has class. The center provides play care."

"Play care?" He reared. "You mean day care? No way."

"It's more of a mother's-morning-out type of thing. Fully licensed workers." Maggie opened her hands. "The children are there only for a few hours at most. The volunteers and staff at the center also use the play care services."

His mother smiled. "That sounds like exactly what we'd need."

Bridger scowled. "You can't be serious."

"It wouldn't be forever, son. Six to seven weeks. The doctors say if we can get Shannon to week thirty-seven, the baby will be considered full-term and will avoid development issues." She snagged hold of his hand. "You'd be with the boys at night."

He shook his head. "I could get called out any hour of the day or night."

Maggie's gaze caught his. And he didn't like how her eyes made his heart accelerate.

"I live right next door. I could help out in those instances, too."

Right next door in the country meant a mile down the road.

"Maggie is good with the boys, son."

Austin and Logan weren't the only ones she'd won over.

GeorgeAnne became brisk. "You must get on the road soon if you want to reach Fayetteville before dark, Wilda." She threw him a look. "Between Maggie and me, all your boys will be taken care of, I promise."

He bristled. He didn't need anybody taking care of him. Yet right now, the truth was, the boys shouldn't be his mother's primary concern.

They were his responsibility. And until he could make more permanent arrangements, Maggie's offer to take care of the twins was a Godsend.

"Unless—" Maggie's lips thinned "—you have a personal objection to me caring for the boys."

Far from it. The opposite of objection, actually. That was what made him wary and hesitant.

He blew out a breath. "Thank you, Maggie. I hate to impose on you—"

"You're not imposing."

He pinched the bridge of his nose. "If you're sure you want to do this—"

"I'm sure." She gave him a tremulous smile. A smile that caused his heart to slam against his breastbone. "Do we have a deal?"

He rested his hands on the top of his gun belt. "Let's see how it goes for a few days."

"It's going to be great. And fun." She smiled. "Can we tell them now?"

The boys appeared thrilled at the chance to spend more time with Maggie.

But the prospect of seeing the vibrant young woman on a daily basis caused his pulse to leap. Not a good thing. Not good at all.

He glanced at her. She had an arm around each of the twins. And he resolved to keep his relationship with the fitness instructor strictly business.

Though when it came to Maggie Arledge, that was a task easier said than done.

Chapter Three

Maggie followed Wilda's minivan to their house. Bridger was called back to the office, but she assured him she was free to watch the boys until he returned home that evening.

Through the trees, she spotted the glint of the blue tin roof. Built at the turn of the last century, the renovated white farmhouse provided a pleasing complement to the spots of pink mountain laurel dotting the ridge above the farm.

Wilda gave her a quick tour of the house. Cardboard boxes littered the family room. "I don't move as fast as I used to." She sighed. "I haven't had time to unpack all the moving boxes."

Maggie patted her arm. "Don't worry about anything but getting to Shannon. Leave everything else to me. The twins will be fine."

Tears winked from her eyes. "Thank you, my dear." Her voice hitched. "I don't know how I would cope if you weren't here."

Just then, a little voice said, "Me hungwy."

"Me, too."

Their grandmother's gaze flitted to Maggie.

She smiled. "You go pack. I'll take care of these hungry young men." She knelt beside the boys. "Would you two help me get lunch together?"

Wilda raised her eyebrows. "Land of lakes, aren't you the brave one?"

Laughing, Maggie shooed her toward the bedrooms. Austin and Logan proved extremely helpful. Or at least, eager to be of help.

Austin pulled out a loaf of bread from the pantry. Logan pointed her to the cabinet that held their plastic cups. She found sandwich fixings in the fridge. With such excellent helpers, in their excitement only a few carrots landed on the floor instead of their plates.

She hoisted the boys into their booster seats at the rustic farm table. With Austin and Logan occupied with their lunch, she went in search of their grandmother.

"You're okay with following the twins' schedule, aren't you?" Pulling clothes from a dresser, Wilda paused. "We're not rigid about it, but after all the changes they've been through in recent months…"

That was the second time she'd remarked on their adjustment to *changes*. Had the move to Truelove upended their little lives so much?

Maggie nodded. "I think everyone can benefit from structure and routine. Especially two-year-olds."

"Almost two-year-olds." Slumping, Wilda sank onto the edge of the bed. "Am I making a mistake in leaving them? They've been through so much. And I won't be able to be here for their birthday."

Maggie felt like she was missing some vital piece of information Wilda apparently assumed she knew but that she didn't.

"I promise you I will do everything in my power on this end to make their birthday wonderful."

Wilda squeezed her hand. "You really are something special, Maggie Arledge. I can't tell you how blessed I feel to have you taking care of the twins." She exhaled. "Bridger is still finding his way with them. Having you here will allow me to concentrate on Shannon and not worry about them."

Finding his way?

Wilda's voice held untold reservations regarding her son's relationship with the boys. There'd been no opportunity for Maggie to observe Bridger with his sons. Perhaps he wasn't the kind of man who connected well with children. GeorgeAnne had said the chief was single.

But what did that mean? Never married? Widowed? Separated? Or divorced? And where was their mother?

Maybe he'd only recently assumed parental custody.

That might explain the veiled references to what the boys had been through. Poor things. Had something happened to their mother? Her heart squeezed.

"Magwee!"

"Magwee!"

Wilda pushed off the mattress. "Your fan club is calling."

"They're going to miss you."

Wilda clicked the suitcase shut. "Not as much as I'll miss them. But we can talk on the phone. I'll have to learn how to do that face-chat thing."

"FaceTime." Maggie's mouth curved. "For sure."

The next thirty minutes were a whirlwind. Somehow Austin managed to get jelly in his hair. She packed a to-go lunch for Wilda. Then Logan needed to go to the potty.

"Oh, no." Wilda's shoulders sagged. "I forgot to tell you, we're in the middle of potty training."

A not so tiny bit of panic flickered in her chest. She'd heard enough from Callie to know potty training was tough. And weren't boys generally harder to train than girls? What had she gotten herself into?

Lord, it's me, Maggie. Help...

Wilda looked on the verge of dissolving into tears.

She took a deep breath. "Show me what to do for Logan. Then text me anything else I need to know."

With rest time next on their schedule, she and Maggie put them in their room with a book.

"They don't have to go to sleep, but they do have to stay on their beds for at least thirty minutes," Wilda explained. "And oftentimes despite themselves, they both fall asleep and I get to enjoy another cup of tea."

Wilda kept her goodbye short so as not to unduly upset the twins.

She walked Wilda onto the gray-planked front porch and out to the minivan.

Then she surprised Maggie by throwing her arms around her. "Thank you, dearest Maggie."

"You're most welcome." She smiled. "I'm going to sound like your mother, but please call or text me to let us know you arrived safely."

"You, Maggie Arledge, are a jewel. Are the men in Truelove blind not to have snapped you up before now?"

That was a topic best left alone.

She tucked a stray tendril of hair behind her ear. "I'll be praying for your daughter."

Wilda nudged her chin toward the house. "I'll be praying for you." She hopped into the van. "Oh, and one more thing I forgot to mention. The boys need a lot of reassurance during thunderstorms. The loud sounds terrify them. Too much like—" A sheen of tears glazed her eyes. "I—I'd better go."

With a small wave, she cranked the engine and steered toward the road.

Maggie wondered what she'd started to say. But shaking her head, she returned to the house. The kitchen wasn't going to clean itself. Tiptoeing down the hall, she risked peeking in on the twins.

Both lay sprawled fast asleep on their beds. Austin clutched a small red fire engine in his hand. A book poked out from beneath Logan's belly.

Caring for the boys might be the hardest job she'd ever taken on. But without a doubt, it would be the toughest job she'd ever love.

When Bridger pulled up to the house after work, he heard laughter coming from the backyard. He rounded the corner of the farmhouse to find Maggie playing with the boys.

Using found objects, she'd erected a makeshift obstacle course in the grass. Austin leapfrogged from one stepping-stone to the next. Logan walked carefully across what appeared to be a two-by-four plank of wood.

At the sight of her, he couldn't stop the quick stab of emotion that flashed through him. Truth was he liked her. Far more than their limited acquaintance warranted. He was attracted to her outgoing nature. Her confidence in herself. The genuineness.

Not wanting to startle her again, he scuffed his feet against the gravel to alert her to his presence. "Hi."

She looked up. "Boys, look who's home."

Home. Something inside his chest twisted painfully. He hadn't considered any place or anyone home since he'd left his parents' house years ago to go to college and then the police academy.

For a time, when he and Chelsea were engaged, he'd believed they'd create a home together someday. And look how that had turned out.

More than anything, he wanted the twins to know what it meant to belong somewhere. The knot in his gut pulled tighter. Was he looking for the same thing, too?

He wasn't comfortable depending on anyone but himself. During his undercover days, that was an unfortunate but necessary fact of life. But for the first time in a long while, he considered reaching for a life outside law enforcement.

Maggie was not only someone worth getting to know, but she might possibly be someone with whom he could finally lower his guard and be himself.

Per his nature, Austin rushed to greet him. Concentrating hard on not falling off the board, Logan merely grunted to acknowledge his uncle's presence.

A good reminder of what was at stake. The well-being and happiness of the twins. Recalling his responsibilities, he pulled back from the edge of no return. If it came to a choice between his heart and theirs, their hearts would come first every time.

Moving to Truelove was about making a new life for the boys. No matter how winsome, Maggie Arledge was a distraction he didn't need.

Reaching the end of the wooden beam, Logan jumped. It was only a five-inch drop. Nevertheless, arms extended and knees flexed, he stuck the landing like an Olympian.

His brown eyes flicked to see if they were watching. "I did it, Magwee. I did it." His usually somber features shone with pride.

Austin fist-pumped the air. "Hoo-way! Hoo-way for Wogan."

She grinned at Bridger. "I love how supportive they are of each other."

He did, too. No matter how confusing the last four months had been for the twins, they'd had each other. He suspected it would always be that way between them.

Logan squatted on the sidewalk to observe a caterpillar. Austin headed toward the screened porch steps.

Bridger started forward at the same instant Maggie did, too. "Careful, Austin…"

"If you're going to go up and down the steps, Austin—" she pointed "—hold on to the rail, please."

He and Maggie positioned themselves where they could lend emergency assistance if needed to either twin.

She smiled. "I hear the twins have a birthday coming up next month."

He pushed the brim of his hat higher. "The sixteenth."

The oddest look passed over her face. "June 16?"

Bridger nodded. "Seems like yesterday they were born."

Her eyes clouded as if with remembered pain.

"Yoo-hoo!"

They turned.

Clutching a sheaf of papers and a large zippered casserole tote, GeorgeAnne bustled into the backyard. "Dinner, as promised. And the application to process your rec membership, Chief Hollingsworth."

Maggie gasped out loud.

GeorgeAnne frowned. "What is it?"

"N-nothing." But she'd blanched. Shadows darkened her expressive brown eyes. "I—I have to go."

He took a step toward her. "Maggie—"

"I—I'll see you tomorrow morning."

Fleeing with an almost frantic haste, Maggie dashed around the corner of the house and out of sight.

GeorgeAnne's nostrils flared. "Did you say something to upset her?" Her voice rose.

"No." He frowned. "I don't know what just happened."

GeorgeAnne pursed her lips. "Perhaps she didn't feel well, or suddenly remembered somewhere she had to be."

He called the boys to come inside for dinner.

Austin poked out his lip. "Where Magwee? Me want Magwee."

Logan pulled on Bridger's sleeve. "Magwee 'morrow?"

He scrubbed his chin. "I think so." He sure hoped so.

GeorgeAnne jutted her jaw. "Of course Maggie will be here tomorrow. Bright and early as agreed." But a bemused expression crossed her wrinkled features. "I'll check on her later. But she's not likely to miss the chance to spend time with *those* boys."

Bridger cut his eyes at the older woman. *Those boys?* What was that supposed to mean?

He reminded himself not to imagine criminal intent behind every statement. Just because he'd been fooled by one pretty face in the past didn't mean all women weren't to be trusted.

Yet Maggie's odd behavior had succeeded in rousing his curiosity. A little skepticism was healthy. With the built-in hazards of his profession, caution and an innate sense of self-preservation had kept him alive thus far.

Once he got the boys in bed tonight, he intended to do a thorough background check on Maggie Arledge. Despite the urgent family crisis, it was something he should have done before he put the twins into her care. It had often proved wiser to assume guilt first. And then be pleasantly surprised if that someone proved innocent.

A slanted lens through which to view life, to be sure, but when it came to the welfare of the twins, now might not be the best time to change his standard operating procedure.

Especially when it concerned the woman who was bringing to life all kinds of feelings he hadn't felt in a long time.

Scarcely aware of having driven the country road between their farms, Maggie arrived home in a daze. She was relieved to find her father's truck missing from the garage.

Resting her forehead against the steering wheel, she squeezed her eyes shut. Was she imagining a connection that didn't exist? But there was no imagining the new police chief's last name.

Truelove's new police chief was Bridger *Hollingsworth*. A coincidence? Maybe. But was it also a coincidence that Austin and Logan's birthday was June 16?

Just like—

Her eyes flew open. Just like her twins. Two boys. Who were the right age. With the exact birthday.

Yet how could she be sure?

Leaning over the seat, she dug through her gym bag. Pawing through the contents, she searched for the printout of the students registered for her classes. Pulling out the folder containing the attendance rosters, she flipped the pages until she reached the Tumbling Tot class.

With her finger, she scanned through the list of names, stopping at the *H*s. *Austin Hollingsworth. Logan Hollingsworth.* Her heart pounded. There was no mistake.

She remembered now it was Callie who'd taken the check-in paperwork from Wilda at church. The older woman had introduced herself and the twins only by their given names.

Outside church that day, her father had called her over to meet the new chief, Bridger. She'd assumed *Bridger* was his last name. And when chancing upon him at the diner—because they'd already sort of, though not quite, met—he hadn't offered his surname.

But he was Bridger Hollingsworth. His mother, Wilda Hollingsworth. And the boys... She clutched the papers to her chest.

The twins—*her* twins—were Austin and Logan Hollingsworth.

Wonder. Delight. Perplexity. A host of conflicting emotions surged through her mind.

Stunned, she got out of the car. Inside the house, she dropped onto the sofa. A huge boulder of emotion clogged her throat. How could this be? And yet it was true. Austin and Logan were her sons.

Part of her was overjoyed. Her maternal feelings for the two boys suddenly made sense. After all this time, to be able to hug her children. To get to know their budding personalities. An opportunity she'd never believed possible.

Yet Austin and Logan crossing her path in remote Truelove couldn't have been an accident. *Right, God? What is going on here?*

But despite her heart trilling with joy, she was also confused and concerned. She had so many unanswered questions.

How had her children come to be under Bridger's care? What had happened to the adoptive parents she'd carefully selected?

She'd been adamant with the small adoption agency. She'd wanted a two-parent household for the twins. A loving home. Financially stable parents who were regular churchgoers.

What had gone wrong? Where were Dana and Jeff Hollingsworth? On paper, they'd been everything she'd hoped for in an adoptive couple.

Totally shaken, she went into her bedroom. Sitting at her desk, she opened her laptop. She wasn't a police chief's daughter for nothing. After typing *Jeff Hollingsworth, Atlanta* into the search engine, she soon found the answer to some of her questions.

Clicking on a link, she pulled up a newspaper article detailing a shooter incident at an Atlanta mall four months ago. With the open-air shopping center crowded with families, a lone gunman had entered the food court, intending to kill as many people as possible. There'd been four casualties. Two women. A teenager. And a man.

She covered her mouth with her hand.

The teenager had been working behind the burger counter. An older woman had been standing in line to order.

Jeff Hollingsworth, an off-duty Georgia state trooper, had run toward the shooter, trying to stop him. His wife had thrown herself over the double stroller containing their twenty-month-old twin sons to protect them.

Tears rolled unchecked across Maggie's face.

Jeff Hollingsworth had succeeded in stopping the killer. Saving countless lives. But lost his own life as a consequence of his heroic actions.

Maggie touched her finger to the photo on the screen of Dana and Jeff in happier times that accompanied the article. Tears blurred her vision. They'd given their lives to save their boys.

She hadn't chosen wrong. They were exactly the people she'd believed them to be and more. She put her head in her hands.

The twins had seen the only mother and father they'd ever known killed in front of them. How traumatized they must have been. But what had happened to them after the shooting?

How had they come from Atlanta to Truelove? What was the connection with Bridger?

Finding Jeff's online obituary, she scanned to the end, where it listed next of kin.

Jeff Hollingsworth was survived by his mother—Wilda Hollingsworth of Raleigh, North Carolina. A sister, Shannon, and her husband, living in Fayetteville. A niece and nephew. Maggie skimmed over their names. And a younger brother—Bridger, a detective with the Raleigh PD.

The pieces of the puzzle fell into place.

What had she been thinking to choose a law enforcement family for her sons? But she knew. She'd been thinking of someone to keep her boys safe from the kind of violence that resulted in their conception.

She'd also been looking for a good man, like her own father, to be a role model to her children.

Through no fault of their own, the parents she'd chosen for the twins had lost their lives. In the aftermath, apparently Bridger had been given guardianship of Austin and Logan.

She ached for the grief Wilda must carry inside her. For the loss Bridger must feel, too.

But since she really knew nothing of Bridger's character, she couldn't shake her worry. Single, just as her aunt had said. No spouse was listed beside his name in the obituary.

She swiped the moisture off her cheeks.

It shouldn't be too hard to find out more about Bridger. The town council had done an extensive background check on him before hiring him as the new police chief.

Her father could fill in many of the blanks in Bridger's life. But it wouldn't do to ask too many questions. She'd have to be careful not to give the small-town grapevine—especially the matchmakers like her great-aunt—the wrong idea.

Maggie pressed her fingers to her temples. "I thought I was doing the right thing in giving up my children, God," she whispered.

She'd been so troubled. Sick at heart. It had taken a great deal of counseling to overcome what had happened to her in Atlanta.

Maggie had been in no shape to care for her babies. Before her pregnancy began to show, she'd quit her job at the investment firm. So, she'd had no means of providing for the twins.

She'd never wanted to be separated from her babies.

But she'd also feared if she somehow managed to keep them close, one day they'd discover the awful circumstances of their conception. She wouldn't—couldn't—risk damaging them in the future with that terrible revelation.

Better for them to be raised by people with no baggage. Free to love and provide for them. Above all else, she wished for them a happy, safe childhood.

She'd given her sons to the Hollingsworths because she loved them. Yet here she was face-to-face with another unforeseen consequence of her wrenching choice.

Not unseen to God, though. None of this was a surprise to Him. She bit her lip at the quiet urging to trust God with everything.

Yet trust didn't come easy for her since that horrible night. She had a hard time trusting herself, much less Bridger, a relative stranger.

She got up fron the desk and stretched out on the bed. "What should I do now, God?" She stared at the ceiling.

What *could* she do? Per the adoption agreement, she'd relinquished her rights to the twins. Was there any recourse left to her?

That was a question best answered by an attorney. No local lawyers specialized in adoptions, but in Asheville, about an hour's drive on the interstate, there were attorneys who did. Tomorrow, she'd make a few phone calls.

Rolling over onto her stomach, she buried her face in the pillow. *Don't think about that night. Don't think about what your life would've been like if you'd made a different decision about your babies.* Only pain lay at the end of the what-ifs.

Maggie was strong now. Capable. She'd never be anyone's victim again.

She clasped her hands under her chin. "Father God, p-please…" Her voice wobbled. "Please help me make sure my children will be all right."

Chapter Four

Reeling from her discovery and needing to clear her head, Maggie went for an early-evening run through the woods at the back of her dad's property.

What was she going to do now?

It was dusk when she returned to find GeorgeAnne's truck in the driveway. The house was dark. Her father must be out for the evening. Her aunt, however, waited for her on the porch.

GeorgeAnne folded her arms against the cool breeze coming off the mountain. "Did something happen at the Hollingsworths' this afternoon to upset you?"

Sweat dotting her forehead, she stared at her great-aunt. Upset? The understatement of the decade.

GeorgeAnne pinched her lips together. "I hoped being around twins that age might provide some comfort. But if seeing them is going to dredge up terrible memories, I can find someone else to take care of the boys."

"No!"

GeorgeAnne jolted.

She bit her lip. That had come out way louder and more vehement than she'd intended.

"I mean…" Gulping, she glanced away toward the sun beginning its descent behind the mountain. What *did* she mean?

GeorgeAnne's face softened. "I've not missed how hard Mother's Day is for you, honey."

Her aunt was giving her a way out. She could bow out of their lives, keep her secret safe forever and still keep track of them, but from a distance.

That was the wisest course of action.

But that was not what her heart had cried out for in those long, lonely hours in the middle of the night when she ached to see her beautiful children. Yearning for the chance to hold them one more time.

There had to be a reason God had practically dropped this opportunity in her lap. So why was she hesitating?

If she continued to take care of the twins until their grandmother returned, she'd not only have the chance to spend time with her children, but also allay her worries regarding Bridger's fitness to parent them.

So was this development a gift? Or an exercise in impending doom?

Perspiration trickled down her neck.

"You've made so much progress getting your life together." Behind the black frames, GeorgeAnne's eyelids drooped. "I couldn't bear the idea of you suffering an emotional setback."

"I—I won't, Aunt G."

GeorgeAnne touched her papery palm to Maggie's cheek. "Are you sure you're up for taking care of the boys?"

Her eyes welled. "I—I am."

"Then what is it, honey? What's wrong?"

"It's just…" A tear made a silent trek down her

cheek. "Suppose I can't bear it? Seeing them every day. Losing them again."

"Again?" Eyes narrowing, GeorgeAnne dropped her hand. "Is there something going on I'm not understanding?"

Her heart hammered.

GeorgeAnne had no way of knowing Austin and Logan were actually her sons. And she couldn't know. No one must ever learn the truth.

"I—I mean I'm afraid of getting attached to Austin and Logan. And when Wilda returns, stepping out of their lives."

GeorgeAnne's brow furrowed. "Perhaps you should pray about taking on their care. I can watch them tomorrow until you decide."

"No." She straightened. "I'm okay to take care of them."

She didn't need to pray. Who better to care for them than their mother? Since handing her babies to the social worker in Atlanta two years ago, she realized now she'd been doing nothing but praying. Her prayers too deep for words. The cry of her heart to one day be reunited with her boys.

The current situation was not of her making. She'd done nothing to interfere in their lives, but here they were in her life again. Austin and Logan in Truelove was the answer to her longing to know them. So why not enjoy the time she'd been offered with the boys?

GeorgeAnne's shrewd eyes probed her face. "Are you sure this is what you want?" Normally resolute, the old woman's chin quivered. "Maybe this is a mistake."

Her heart skipped a beat. "It isn't a mistake." Had her emotions given her away? "This is what I want."

"Or…" GeorgeAnne cocked her head. "Perhaps I've misread the situation."

Her lungs constricted. Had her aunt guessed the truth?

"Maybe it's Bridger, and not the boys, who has you in such a tizzy?"

She opened her mouth and then closed it.

"It also hasn't escaped my notice that being around men makes you nervous. But when I saw you two at the diner, you seemed so at ease." GeorgeAnne put her arm around Maggie's shoulders. "His undercover work with the dregs of society has made him somewhat rough around the edges. But I won't allow him to frighten—"

"No, Aunt G."

It wasn't right for GeorgeAnne to get the wrong impression about him.

At the rec center when he tried to steady her, she'd been startled. But only because she was caught off guard. He hadn't meant to scare her.

He'd been trying to keep Austin from knocking her to the ground. Once she stopped flashing back to that night, she'd seen the sincerity in his face. And for once, the fear hadn't taken root. It had been something of a revelation.

"Bridger's been nothing but honorable." She squared her shoulders. "Leave him to me."

"Well, now…" GeorgeAnne's mouth quirked. "I was hoping you'd say that."

She frowned at her aunt.

GeorgeAnne gave her a wide-eyed look of innocence. "What?"

Sharp-tongued, bossy and brusque, *innocence* wasn't the first word that sprang to mind when it came to her aunt and her meddling machinations.

GeorgeAnne fluttered her hand. "All's well that ends well, honey."

She rolled her eyes. "Or do you mean all's fair in love and war?"

"Love." GeorgeAnne winked. "I like the way you're thinking, Mary Margaret."

She buttoned her lip. Least said, soonest mended. Prosecuting attorneys could've learned a thing or two from her matchmaking aunt.

Still, no one could ever learn about her relationship with the twins. Not her beloved aunt. Most especially not Chief Hollingsworth.

She had the impression—perhaps because of his undercover work?—he wasn't a man who trusted easily. And if he ever suspected the truth, she feared he'd never allow her within a mile of the twins.

She'd always lived her life in a straightforward manner. And naively expected others to do the same. But that night in Atlanta had forever cured her of that delusion.

Deception didn't come naturally and left her feeling off-kilter. As off-kilter as Bridger made her feel when he looked at her with those intense blue eyes of his.

But she refused to lose this chance to know her boys. No matter what it took to make this work. Because GeorgeAnne was right.

When it came to her children, all was fair in love and war. Did that mean she was at war with Bridger Hollingsworth? At least, not yet. Hopefully, he'd never learn her true relationship to his nephews.

But no matter what, despite the sparks of electricity between them, she wasn't going to let the police chief—or anyone else—ever keep her from her children again.

* * *

Bridger studied the info he'd pulled up on his laptop. After GeorgeAnne's delicious meal, the boys had fallen into bed.

He should feel guilty about doing a background check on the lovely Maggie Arledge, but he didn't. He would have done the same on anyone in daily proximity to the boys.

And after what happened with her earlier in the backyard, he had doubts aplenty regarding her trustworthiness. She'd been so friendly.

Until she wasn't.

Like a proverbial door slamming in his face. Raising a drawbridge, she shut him out. He had no explanation for the strange vibe he'd sensed emanating from her.

He scrubbed his forehead. What had they been talking about that could have possibly set her off? Best he recalled, they'd been talking about the twins and their shenanigans.

Snap decisions were not his preferred modus operandi. Yet he understood his mother well enough to know she'd agree to leave for Fayetteville only if he immediately hired Maggie to look after the boys. Seeing no other recourse to getting his mom to his sister, he'd reluctantly agreed.

Now, though, he was second-guessing himself. He couldn't forget the weird incident with Maggie. Fine one minute, then hurrying away the next. In his line of work, only the guilty ran. Behind the sweet smile and dancing dark eyes, she could be emotionally unstable. Possibly unfit to care for the twins.

Thinking of his ex-fiancée, Chelsea, he'd had his fill

of women with integrity issues. He was nobody's fool. Once had been enough.

Gritting his teeth, he scrolled through various social media outlets. She appeared not to have much of an online presence. What did that say about her? That she didn't walk around with her head stuck in her phone all day? Since she'd be responsible for the twins' welfare, that was a good thing. Or was it?

What deeper significance might her lack of engagement actually imply? Was she hiding something? Should he be suspicious?

He scanned the screen, reviewing the facts he'd been able to ascertain. She'd been born in Truelove. Twenty-eight years old. Graduated from a North Carolina university with a degree in communications.

She spent a few years working with a large financial institution in Atlanta. But then two years ago, she'd completed an associate degree from the community college not far from Truelove and become certified as a fitness instructor.

Why the abrupt career change?

Perhaps she missed her father. Maybe she disliked the noise and stress of living in the big city. Or she didn't like her job.

His mother and the twins believed Maggie was the best thing since air-conditioning hit the humid South. Should he give her the benefit of the doubt? GeorgeAnne could've been right about her niece feeling unwell earlier.

Maybe *he* was the problem, not Maggie. Imagining problems where none existed. Borrowing trouble. Too hypervigilant.

Yet there'd also been another red flag at the recreation center that morning. Her overreaction to his touch on her shoulder. Perhaps the only problem was she didn't like him. Maybe he made her uncomfortable.

As he glared at the monitor, his gut twisted. Because despite his reservations about her, he liked her. Something about her made him want to ditch his cynicism and take a chance on finding love again. But the response she evoked within him was the very thing he must guard against.

No matter his feelings for Maggie, he couldn't afford to bury his head in the sand of a lovely illusion with no basis in reality. He'd made that mistake with Chelsea.

"God," he whispered, "what should I do?"

Slumped in the chair, he quieted himself. Praying for wisdom. Waiting for direction.

After a while, he received a strong impression of what he should do. Wait.

He scrubbed his hand over his beard stubble, a holdover from his undercover days.

Okay, then... That was what he would do. He'd keep his concerns to himself. But in addition to waiting, he'd also keep watch.

For the sake of the twins. His own sake, too.

The next morning, as agreed, at 6:15 a.m., Maggie arrived at the Hollingsworth home.

At her knock, Bridger unlocked the back door off the screened porch.

"Morning, Maggie," he rasped in a gravelly first-thing-in-the-morning voice.

Her heart sped up a little. "Morning."

Ushering her inside the kitchen, he raked his hand over his mussed, just-got-out-of-bed hair. Butterflies fluttering in her stomach, she dropped her eyes to be safe. Her gaze landed on his bare feet poking out from his blue jeans.

She flushed.

He must have just gotten out of bed, pulled on a pair of jeans and a T-shirt. Of course, those swimming pool–blue eyes of his were a no-go zone. She decided to train her eyes on a spot in the middle of his forehead. But Bridger Hollingsworth had an attractive forehead, too.

She sighed.

His attractive forehead creased. "I appreciate your willingness to start your day with the boys so early, but I could get them up before you arrive."

She set her purse on the counter. "I'm glad to do it."

In fact, she wanted to be the first person they saw when they woke up each day. She wanted to enjoy their tousled hair. The still-drowsy smiles. And be the recipient of their I'm-so-glad-to-see-you hugs. Not that she could explain that to their uncle and now-legal guardian.

His eyes narrowed. "I'm capable of getting them out of bed, feeding them and dressing them."

Bridger seemed different with her today. His manner less at ease. Almost suspicious. But after the way she'd behaved yesterday afternoon, she couldn't fault his skepticism.

"I—I know." Taking a quick breath, she thought fast. "But this gives you time to get ready before heading into the station."

One of the by-products of being a police chief's daughter? She knew the subtle body language cues that cops were trained to pick up on.

So raising her gaze, she didn't look away or fidget under his scrutiny. "I truly don't mind."

He stared at her, puzzlement written across his features as if he couldn't quite figure her out. But after a moment, he nodded. "I don't want to take advantage of your good nature."

She'd made it a habit of life to always tell the truth. Duplicity didn't come easily, nor sit well with her. Guilt pierced her conscience. It wasn't so much him taking advantage of her as the other way around.

"Go." She motioned. "Enjoy the peace and quiet for a few more minutes. I've got the boys."

Eyes crinkling, he gave her a crooked smile.

Her knees wobbled. *Be still, my heart.* Perhaps it was a good thing he didn't smile at her more often.

As he disappeared down the hallway, she began putting breakfast together. With Bridger awake and moving around, it wouldn't be long before the twins would be up and at 'em.

Sure enough, she soon heard the twins stirring in their bedroom. Leaving the coffee percolating, she ventured down the hall and cracked open the door. Both boys lay sprawled on top of the covers of their respective beds.

As soon as he spotted her in the doorway, Austin bounced up. "Magwee!" A print of a big rig covered the shirt of his orange-and-black toddler pajamas.

Logan gave her a slow smile that wrenched her heart.

Flinging himself off the bed, Austin wrapped himself around her legs.

She planted a kiss on top of his blond curls. "Hello, my sleepy sweethearts." Taking him into her arms, she carried him over to Logan's bed.

Her shyer child waited for his turn to be noticed. On her watch, he would always be. And no less loved.

In red, white and blue pajamas, Logan's top sported trains and the words *All Aboard* emblazoned across his chest.

Sinking onto the mattress, she shifted Austin over to one arm so she could enfold Logan with her other arm. "Good morning, little alligator."

Grinning, he climbed into her lap and clasped his arms around her neck. Closing her eyes, she inhaled the scent of baby shampoo, the clean, soapy aroma from his bath the night before, and little boy smell of him.

Thank You, God. Thank You for this.

If she lived to be a hundred, this would be the memory she'd hold of her children forever. Her arms and her heart full of them.

Letting go, Logan took both sides of her face into his small palms. "Hungwy, Magwee."

Crawling off the bed, Austin tugged at her hand. "Hungwy, Magwee."

She laughed.

The boys were already bottomless pits. Good thing Bridger had a reliable income. Give or take a decade, the twins would be eating him out of house and home.

She inched off the mattress. "Let's eat breakfast, shall we?"

Austin fist-pumped the air. "Hoo-way!"

Logan clambered onto the floor. "Yay!"

They raced past her. Their bare feet pattered down the hall to the kitchen. She hurried to catch up.

At the farmhouse table, Austin and Logan climbed unassisted into their booster seats. When their uncle joined them, they were already making short work of their blueberry yogurt.

As she stirred the oatmeal on the stove, her heart lurched at his nearness.

He sniffed the air. "Is that coffee?"

She gestured toward the coffeemaker. "I figured you would want some caffeine before you headed out." She ladled the oatmeal into an earthenware bowl. "And some oatmeal to tide you over till lunch."

His shoulders relaxed a notch. "This is awfully nice of you, Maggie. You didn't have to… I don't expect you to…" He shuffled his feet.

Maggie placed the bowl on the table. "This batch of oatmeal is more than even those two bottomless pits could eat in one sitting."

Spoon in hand, Logan looked up. "What's bottom pit, Magwee?" Yogurt smeared in a near perfect ring around his mouth and on his chin, he resembled a pint-size Santa.

"Good thing you put bibs on them." Bridger tapped his finger against his temple. "Future note to self."

She kissed the top of Logan's head. "*You* are the bottomless pit."

Austin waved his spoon. "Me pit, too, Magwee?"

Bridger laughed. "You, too, Austin."

They shared a look. And in that split second it was as if something tilted in her world. As if Earth faltered on its axis before righting itself.

Bridger poured himself a cup of coffee and took a sip. "Thanks again."

She divided the rest of the oatmeal between the boys' smaller cereal bowls. "No problem."

"Aren't you going to eat any breakfast?"

She shook her head. "I had a protein bar already."

He reached for another mug hanging on a small peg

underneath the cabinet. "Can I at least pour you a cup of coffee?"

She glanced from the boys to the stove and back again. "I shouldn't…"

"My mother's been gone less than twenty-four hours, but already I'm craving adult conversation." He pulled out a chair. "Please? I'd appreciate the company."

The smart thing would be to avoid spending any more time than she had to with Chief Hollingsworth. Sooner or later, she was bound to trip herself up somehow. But then his gaze locked on to hers. Her pulse leaped.

It ought to be a crime to have eyes as blue as his.

Knees suddenly weak, she sat down. "Okay," she said in a soft voice.

"Wonderful." A smile lit his usually unreadable countenance. "Cream? Sugar? Both?"

"Cr-cream only."

Her cheeks grew warm. What was it about this man that made her go all tongue-tied and inarticulate? She cleared her throat. "Actually, I prefer a little coffee with my cream."

Holding the carafe over the cup, he paused. "I'll fill the mug only three-quarters."

She leaned forward. "Thanks." She rested her palms on the tabletop. "My one indulgence."

He gave her an admiring glance. "Can't say it's done you any harm." He handed her the cup.

She took a quick sip to hide the blush she could feel creeping from beneath the collar of her lilac exercise top.

He sat across from her and for the next few minutes in between bites, he updated her on the latest news from his mom. It was almost… Maggie struggled to identify the feeling.

Cozy. That was what it was. Like they'd been sharing breakfast forever. No big deal.

Tell that to the butterflies playing tag in her belly. *Get a grip, Mags. What is your deal with him?*

She traced her finger around the rim of the mug. "I'm glad to hear your sister is doing better."

"Knowing my usually energetic sister, bed rest is probably making her stir-crazy." He took a swig of coffee. "She reminds me of you."

Maggie blinked. "Me?"

He rose. "I get the feeling you don't let any grass grow under your feet."

Scudding back her chair, she quickly removed the twins' now-empty bowls from their reach. They'd decided to play bumper bowls with each other. "The boys will keep me on my toes."

"Definitely." Rinsing out his own bowl, he threw her an amused look over his shoulder. "Until I got them corralled into bed last night, they ran me off my feet. I've expended less energy in a foot chase with criminals."

While he finished getting ready for work, she removed the plastic bibs from the boys' necks and cleaned them up. Changing them out of their pajamas, she helped them into jeans and the complementary but not matching shirts she found in the bureau drawer. But amid cries of "Me do, Magwee," her contribution largely amounted to supervision versus hands-on assistance.

On his way out, Bridger caught them in the hall bathroom. She'd squeezed a tiny dot of toothpaste onto each of their toothbrushes. She glanced up at him.

His broad shoulders filled the doorway. The spicy

but pleasing aroma of his aftershave wafted past her nose. He smelled as good as he looked.

She went crimson.

Wasn't like it was her first time around men in uniform. She'd spent her life around police officers. But not this man, who filled out his uniform very nicely.

"Say goodbye to—" She tilted her head. "What do they call you?"

"With the boys living in Georgia until a few months ago, we didn't know each other too well." He leaned his shoulder against the doorframe. "Not sure they actually call me anything."

She clamped her lips together. Exactly what she feared. He was almost as much a stranger to the twins as she was.

He crossed his arms, and the fabric on his shirt stretched over his well-muscled chest. "'Uncle Bridger' would probably be best."

"Tell Uncle Bridger goodbye, boys."

"Bye, Unc Bwridge," Austin said, sucking the toothpaste off the toothbrush.

Maggie took his toothbrush away from him. "Brush your teeth like we practiced, Austin. Don't just suck the—"

Ready to spit, Logan aimed at the sink and missed. "Waiter, gator."

She sighed.

Bridger chuckled. "A work in progress."

She rolled her eyes. "Aren't we all?"

He threw up his hand. "After a while, you crocodiles. I'm out of here." Straightening, he rapped a staccato beat on the doorframe. "Maybe I'll see you in town. You're teaching today, right?"

Maggie handed the toothbrush back to Austin. "Yes, I am."

"So it'd be okay if I stopped by to say hello, wouldn't it?"

Maggie stiffened. Checking up on her? As was his right, she reminded herself. Showing due diligence and everything to be expected from a proper parent.

"That's not a problem is it?" His fabulous eyes darkened. "You don't mind?"

Mind? Why should she mind? Just one more opportunity to give herself away…

She should be ecstatic at his protectiveness toward the twins. Even if it rankled, his caution was commendable. Trust was a two-way street, and had to be earned. She of all people totally got that.

"It's great." She rubbed her mouth, stopping midswipe. One of those guilty-body-signal things. "No problem." She forced a smile. "We'll see you later, then."

Law enforcement officers were some of the smartest, most intuitive people she'd ever known. Somehow she had to figure out a way to ignore the megawatt effect of his smile, lest she betray her real identity.

Because the alternative—losing her children again—was unthinkable.

Chapter Five

Wilda hadn't been kidding about the production involved in getting the boys out the door.

By the time Maggie packed lunches and gathered their backpack, she was cutting it close getting to the rec center in time for her infant class. Twins in tow, she almost made it out to the car…until Logan announced he needed to go potty.

Going inside again, she dumped their stuff—kids had so much stuff—on the kitchen table and ran to help Logan do his business.

It was her own fault for not asking if they had to go before heading out. Like Bridger said, future note to self. Thinking about their uncle made her heart stutter.

Irritation with herself burned at her stomach.

She spent another five minutes coaxing the human pogo stick named Austin to try, too. She nearly had another crisis on her hands when she wrangled them out to the driveway and suddenly remembered by law they were both required to ride in car seats.

But glancing inside her car, she realized that while she might have forgotten, the police chief had remembered. She hadn't bothered to lock her vehicle. And he'd thoughtfully transferred the seats into her car.

She strapped the twins into their seats. Finally, she was able to set off down the curvy mountain road toward town. Her eyes darted to the rearview mirror. The boys happily chatted with each other in the back seat.

Was this what being a mom was like? Barely contained chaos? She smiled at her reflection. If so, she'd take spilled milk and high energy any day, every day.

It was a glorious late-spring morning.

"Let's sing a song," she called. As the car wound its way around the mountain, she plied them with her somewhat off-key rendition of "You Are My Sunshine."

She grimaced. Nobody would ever mistake her for a singer. She'd always been more tomboy athlete. But reunited with her boys, she couldn't contain the joy she felt inside.

At the rec center, Austin went into the play care room without a backward glance. But Logan held on to her leg tightly before GeorgeAnne managed to entice him over to the Lincoln Logs and into the care of one of the workers.

He was already building a wall by the time Maggie turned at the door. Outfitted in her favorite blue velour exercise outfit, GeorgeAnne followed on her heels.

"Thanks for being here, Aunt G."

Her aunt shrugged. "No problem. I thought this being the first full day, they might need help adjusting to a new environment."

So many new adjustments over the short course of their lives. Too many. She hated to leave them.

Maggie gnawed at her lower lip. "Maybe I should cancel my class."

GeorgeAnne patted her arm. "They'll be fine. The Baby Twisters are already arriving."

Still she lingered.

"I'll check on them myself, Mary Margaret. Thirty minutes from now you can see them again before you start your next class."

She released a slow trickle of air between her lips. "I know I'm being ridiculous. It's just…"

GeorgeAnne threw her a sharp look. "It's just what?"

She swallowed. "Nothing. You're right. They don't know me well enough to truly miss me."

Not yet anyway. But when Wilda returned and Maggie's services were no longer required, what then?

Squaring her shoulders, she headed for the small gym. She couldn't—wouldn't—think about that now.

And sure enough when she peeked in on them later, the twins appeared to be coping quite well without her. Squatting on the rug, Logan had managed to build an impressive model of a cabin, using only the picture on the outside of the container as a guide.

"My little engineer," she whispered.

Some flash of movement through the glass door must have caught Austin's attention. Sitting at the table with the other kids, he looked up from the mound of Play-Doh in front of him. He caught sight of her, and his face broke into a wide grin. Her heart melted. Perfectly content, he waved, then smashed his fist into the clay.

"And my little wrecking ball." She chuckled. She could barely tear herself away.

Next up—the Silver Sneaker class. The class was designed to increase muscle strength and improve daily living activities for senior adults.

The matchmaker trio were her most enthusiastic students. Each participant was equipped with a chair for seated exercises and also for standing support during range-of-movement routines.

Afterward, the three ladies gathered outside the play care room to watch Maggie watch the twins. Best of friends, the Double Name Club trifecta also sported a similar taste in exercise attire.

In pink velour, pleasingly plump, never-met-a-stranger ErmaJean smiled. "Such lovely boys."

Clad in lavender velour, former schoolteacher Ida-Lee, the oldest of the matchmakers, inclined her snowy white head. "Adorable."

She cut her eyes at the women, wondering and fearing where this conversation was headed.

When Maggie's friend Amber had married Erma-Jean's grandson, the older woman had also become great-grandmother to Amber's twin girls.

ErmaJean's denim-blue eyes twinkled. "Other than my grandson, I can't think of a handsomer man than our new police chief, Bridger Hollingsworth. Can you, GeorgeAnne?"

With a sly smile, GeorgeAnne planted her hands on her hips. "Which do you prefer, Mary Margaret? A man in a tuxedo, a uniform or a pickup truck?"

Thinking of Bridger earlier that morning, she opened her mouth to reply, but decided not to take her aunt's all-too-obvious bait.

Reaching behind her head, she pulled the ends of her ponytail, tightening the knot. "I'm sure I couldn't say."

GeorgeAnne's lips twitched. She was either having a spasm or highly amused by Maggie's feeble attempt to deflect.

"I haven't seen Chief Hollingsworth in a tuxedo."

Ever helpful, ErmaJean patted Maggie's arm. "But he does have a mighty fine pickup truck."

GeorgeAnne laughed. Although coming from her, it sounded closer to a bark. IdaLee covered her mouth with a blue-veined hand to hide a smile.

Maggie fidgeted. "Would you look at the time?" She reached for the door—and an escape hatch. "I'd better rescue the workers from two hungry boys wanting their lunch."

GeorgeAnne wagged her finger. "You can run, but you can't hide from love forever, Mary Margaret."

Or, apparently, the Truelove matchmakers.

When she reemerged with the boys, thankfully they'd dispersed. No doubt headed to wage mischief and mayhem elsewhere. Still contemplating her brush with the matchmakers, she herded the twins through the sliding glass doors at the entrance.

Those busybodies were probably terrorizing some other poor, innocent, unsuspecting—

Hands on Austin's and Logan's shoulders guiding them forward, she came to an immediate stop.

Arms crossed, their uncle leaned against the hood of his cruiser, parked at the curb. His long, uniform-clad legs stretched out in front of him. Not that she noticed.

He straightened. "Hey, guys."

Never hesitating to hurl himself at any object of his affection, Austin barreled toward his uncle. "I pway wid dough." He caught Bridger around the knees. But feet firmly braced, the police chief absorbed the impact.

Hand atop Austin's curls, he directed his gaze to her. "Maggie."

Something pinged inside her chest. Two syllables.

But the way he said it… She liked the sound of her name on his lips.

Maggie adjusted the strap of the backpack on her shoulder. Mainly to give herself time to recover from the sudden shock—and pleasure—of unexpectedly seeing him.

With Austin clinging to his leg like an anchor, Bridger slogged forward a step. "Hey, Logan." He held out his hand.

But Logan didn't relinquish his hold on her.

Bridger dropped his hand as confusion and hurt flitted across his chiseled features. And she experienced an unwilling sympathy for him. New to parenting, like herself, but he was trying.

Her conscience smote her. Maybe if she would stop being so selfish with the twins, she might find a way to help him connect with Logan.

"Maggie?" Bridger broadened his chest. "I mentioned I might stop by…"

It wasn't like her to go all schoolgirl crush over a man. As for the heart palpitations? Until now, she'd believed them a figment of romance novel imagination. Or an indicator of an impending heart attack.

He rested his hands on his gun belt. "I wanted to take the three of you to lunch at the Jar."

Bridger had nice hands. Large, strong, long-fingered. Manly hands. Yes, okay, she'd noticed.

A crease formed in the space between his eyebrows. Someone ought to tell him not to scowl like that. He was going to end up with a permanent groove in an otherwise extremely handsome face. She fought the irrational urge to smooth away the frown line.

He peered at her. "Did I lose you again?"

She shook herself and unglued her tongue from the roof of her mouth. *Use your words, Mags, or he'll think you a bigger idiot than he already does.*

Maggie motioned toward the wooden table near the strip of woods separating the parking lot from the river. "I made the boys a picnic lunch."

His shoulders drooped. "Oh."

"But I made plenty. If you'd like to join us."

"That would be wonderful." He pushed the brim of his hat with the knuckle of his finger. "Thanks." He gave her a slow, lopsided smile.

She gulped. "Good."

He insisted on carrying the backpack for her. Underneath the somewhat gruff exterior, he was a gentleman. And as the twins' guardian, he'd probably teach them to become gentlemen, too.

Which was good. So why did his proving to be a great guy only add to her dilemma?

He lifted Austin and deposited his nephew onto the wooden bench. Unpacking lunch, she handed Austin his sandwich. Refusing offers of help, Logan clambered onto the wooden bench by himself.

It was becoming harder to justify her continuing distrust of their uncle. If the boys' future hadn't been at stake, she believed perhaps they could've become friends.

Or even more?

She sucked a breath.

Bridger's eyes swept over her. "Anything wrong?" His gaze sent a flutter down to her toes.

She concentrated on handing out the food. "Nope."

A beautiful spring day. Her beloved children. A handsome man. What could possibly be wrong?

Nothing, as long as the very handsome policeman never learned the truth about the secret she was keeping.

After their al fresco lunch, he and Austin wandered down the embankment to the river.

Like his father had shown him and his brother so long ago, Bridger showed Jeff's son how to skip rocks across the surface of the water.

Well, he demonstrated. Austin chucked the rocks into the river.

"Impressive," Maggie called from the picnic table on the rise of land above the river.

Logan squatted beside a dandelion in the grass. He'd refused to accompany his twin and Bridger to the river-bank.

Through the overhanging oak, filtered light dappled sunshine across her dark hair. A play of shadow and light—not unlike Maggie herself.

Lest Austin get the bright idea to throw himself in the water, he guided the small boy back to the table. Austin held his arms up to her, and Maggie pulled him into her lap.

He glanced at Logan. "Obviously, my parenting skills need work."

"I have a feeling parenting is about on-the-job training." She handed Austin a blue sippy cup filled with water. "It will get better."

"Will it?" He sank onto the bench. An unexpected lump grew in his throat. "My brother, Jeff, and his wife, Dana, wanted children for so long. It doesn't seem right it's me enjoying this beautiful day with the twins instead of them."

Her mouth quivered. "They were good people."

Taken aback, he frowned. It sounded as if she knew them. But of course. His brow cleared. After the shooting, she and millions of other Americans had probably seen the news coverage or read about his brother.

"I try to be worthy of the honor they bestowed on me as the boys' guardian." He laid his forearms across the table. "But Jeff is a tough act to follow."

She eased a wriggly Austin to the ground. "I think all anyone can do is just be themselves."

The little boy strolled over to check out what his twin was doing.

"And trust God to supply what we lack." He sighed. "I'm counting on Him."

Her eyes flicked to him.

"Sorry." He lifted his hat and resettled it on his head. "Just being honest."

Her smile faltered.

Bridger rubbed the back of his neck. "You're easy to talk to." Too easy. And the realization unsettled him.

She didn't return the sentiment. Instead, in one fluid motion, she swung her legs over the bench, and rose. She walked toward the boys.

Yet if he'd hoped unburdening himself would elicit personal disclosures on her behalf, he was doomed to disappointment. Being honest with her actually appeared to have had the opposite effect, and he wasn't sure why.

He was a big guy. His dad and Jeff had been, too. Did his size intimidate her?

Skittish, she went out of her way to avoid physical contact with him. The uniform made some people uncomfortable, but that didn't jibe with her former police chief father. She'd been around law enforcement her entire life.

Logan stood up. "Magwee." With a shy smile, he offered her a messy bouquet of wild violets.

Suddenly, as if a light switched on within, her entire face lifted.

For no reason he could pinpoint, disquiet needled him. Resolving to stop thinking like a cop, he pushed aside the signal his gut was trying to send him.

Be thankful you've found someone who obviously loves the boys so much.

Maybe, like his more reserved nephew, she was simply a private person. Either that, or she didn't find him likable. The notion stung.

"Wook, Bwidge!" Bouncing on his tiptoes, Austin held the stem of a downy dandelion in his hand. "Wook at dis one."

Untangling himself from the table, he headed toward his nephew. "I know something fun we can do with that, Austin. Something I did when I was a boy."

Austin waved the seed head in the air between them like a banner. "Yay!"

Logan jerked his head toward Bridger. "Me one, too."

She plucked two more dandelions from the patch of grass. "Here's one for you and me, Logan."

He crouched to the twins' height. "Look what happens when you blow on it, guys."

"Wike dis?" Puckering his lips, Austin puffed, yet little to no air actually exited his mouth.

He smiled. "Good try, but not exactly."

She laughed. "We'll work on their blowing skills so they'll be ready for the candles on their big day."

He made a face. "I don't know anything about throwing a kid's birthday party."

She twisted the silver earring on her earlobe. "I might have a few ideas."

"Great." Picking a dandelion for himself, he held it in front of his face. "And like the candles on a cake, guys, first you close your eyes…"

Clutching the stems, the twins squeezed their eyes shut. He caught her eye. She smiled.

Warmth filled him. "Make a wish you hope will come true, boys."

Almost simultaneously, the twins bounced with anticipation.

"Did you guys make your wish?"

Chubby cheeks engorged with air, the twins bobbed their heads. A teasing smile playing about her lips, she lifted her dandelion in the air as if for a toast.

"You can open your eyes now, Austin and Logan. Everybody ready?"

This was way more fun than lunch in the station break room, or at his desk poring over paperwork.

"On the count of three. One—"

"Four, seven!" Logan shouted.

In a sputter of air and saliva, to the boys' delight, fluff flew everywhere. The twins chased after the floating wisps.

"'Four, seven' works, too." He chuckled. "Okay. Grown-ups' turn."

Blowing the spores, Maggie went first. Then him. A stray bit of fuzz landed on his cheekbone.

Smiling, she touched his face with her fingertips to brush away the fuzz. Pinpricks of awareness skittered down his spine.

Perhaps realizing what she'd done, she widened her eyes. "I'm sorry." She dropped her hand. "I don't usually... I shouldn't have—"

"It's fine."

More than fine actually. The coolness of her hand against his skin had set his heart thudding. Smelling of tangy citrus, her light perfume sent his senses reeling.

Chasing each other in the grass, the boys ran circles around them.

On the nape of her neck, midday heat curled stray tendrils of hair that had escaped her ponytail.

She looked at him, away and then back at him again. "What did you wish for?"

Heat flashed through him. "Can't tell, or it won't come true."

Because what he wished was for more sunny, carefree days with the twins.

And the beautiful twin wrangler, who made him feel hopeful they might actually one day become friends.

Chapter Six

Later that night, Maggie stared at the ceiling above her bed.

In her mind, she went over every nuance of their picnic together. What on earth had possessed her to touch his cheek? What was she thinking?

Groaning, she rolled over and buried her face in the pillow. That was the problem. She hadn't been thinking.

She'd wondered at the feel of the stubble on his jaw. Coarse or soft? When the downy fuzz landed on his cheek, without stopping to think, she'd given in to her curiosity.

Judging by the expression on his face, she'd surprised him. She'd surprised herself. Yet he hadn't seemed bothered, or put out by her gesture. On the contrary, his blue eyes had warmed.

So where did that leave her? Conflicted, she felt a mixture of embarrassment and something she wasn't ready to put a name to yet.

The next day, having gotten very little sleep, she arrived at the Hollingsworth home as usual, but filled with trepidation. He'd given her a key, but after what happened yesterday she felt the need to reestablish boundaries. Raising her hand, she knocked on the door. And waited anxiously, wondering if henceforth, her interaction with Bridger would be awkward.

So, so stupid. Too much was at stake for her to suddenly start feeling something—anything—for Austin and Logan's guardian. The man had the power to deny her access to her sons.

Whatever it was she'd felt—loneliness, chemistry, whatever—nothing was worth jeopardizing losing her time with them.

But, opening the door, he smiled and ushered her inside. Her stomach was in knots. Yet her traitorous heart—that appeared to have abandoned all common sense—couldn't help but note how good he looked. Even first thing in the morning with his hair still damp from a shower.

He retrieved his steaming coffee cup from the kitchen island. "Forgot your key?"

"I didn't want to overstep."

Taking a swallow, he peered at her over the rim of the mug. "Working together so closely for the boys' sake, I'd like us to be friends."

Setting the cup on the countertop, he put his hands in his pockets. Almost as if he were nervous. "Could we be friends?"

His gaze locked on to hers. And again, she felt the electric push-pull, totally messing-with-her-head vibe between them. She reminded herself to breathe.

She nodded. "Friends."

He moved away to finish getting ready for work. Leaving her both relieved that he hadn't uncovered her secret, and yet hungry to spend more time with him.

Yes… She had definitely taken leave of her senses.

Over the next few days, she and the boys fell into a routine. On mornings she didn't teach, she got out the double jogging stroller, and they went for a run on an old, little-used farm road adjacent to the Hollingsworth property.

They'd have lunch at the house, followed by rest time and, later, an afternoon snack. She would have dinner cooking on the stove by the time Bridger arrived home from work.

"Maggie, I don't expect you to prepare meals for us on top of everything else you do for the boys." He placed his hat on a stool at the island. "Speaking of the twins…" He glanced around the kitchen. "Should I be worried that I don't hear them?"

"Normally, yes." She gestured toward the living room. "But earlier this afternoon, we made a tent with the dining room chairs and blankets. I told them if they'd play quietly until dinner, we'd get milkshakes tomorrow after my class."

He rolled his tongue in his cheek. "Bribery, huh?"

She shrugged. "Whatever works."

"Good to know. I'll put that in my parenting tool kit." Unbuttoning his cuffs, he rolled up his sleeves. "I don't want you to feel like you have to put on a meal for us every night."

"I can barely hold off the ravening wolves, otherwise known as your nephews, until you get home every evening."

He grinned. "A good, healthy Hollingsworth appetite."

"If Austin and Logan had to wait to eat until you fixed something…" Protective mitts on her hands, she carefully removed the casserole from the oven and set it on a padded trivet. "Let's just say I couldn't guarantee your safety." She smirked. "For the welfare of our new police chief, fixing dinner is my civic duty."

He laughed. He had a nice laugh. Every time he laughed, she got that melted-butter feeling in her belly.

And she'd made a startling discovery over the course of their first week together. She liked making the usually serious, rather stoic police chief laugh. Made her feel like she had some sort of superpower when it came to him.

Which was ridiculous. When it came to Bridger Hollingsworth, she had nothing. Didn't want anything. Except his nephews.

Don't get emotionally involved. Remember why you're here—to spend time with Austin and Logan.

Yet when she was with their uncle, she had a hard time remembering anything. Including her name.

Removing the oven mitts, she did a quick survey of the kitchen to make sure she hadn't forgotten anything. "I guess that about does it. I'll say good-night to the boys, and then I'll be off."

"Maggie, wait…"

He stepped into her path, causing her to look up at him. And catch her breath.

"You did all this work. It doesn't seem right you don't get to eat it, too. Why don't you join us?" Then he frowned. "Unless you have a date or something."

"I—I…" *Stop stammering.* "I usually fix supper for Dad. No other plans."

Was it her, or had the oxygen in the room suddenly disappeared?

His eyes lit. "Invite your father over. Why don't you both join us?"

Why? Because the more time she spent with Bridger, the more she risked slipping up and giving something away that could ruin this opportunity to know her sons.

She was all set to refuse, but what came out of her mouth was "I'll call him."

He smiled. "I'll get the dining room chairs and make sure the boys wash their hands for supper."

She called her father. He was thrilled at the invitation. She suspected he missed talking law enforcement now that he was retired. Although with the twins, any conversation at the dinner table might prove an uphill battle.

It was only while setting out two more place settings that she realized despite her constant proximity to the new police chief, she hadn't felt afraid. Not once. On the contrary, there was something rather reassuring and comforting about Bridger Hollingsworth.

Friends... Just friends, Mags.

Sure, but tell that to her heart.

Although he tried to set aside Saturday as a day for just him and the twins, Bridger received a call from Dispatch regarding an ongoing domestic situation at a trailer on the outskirts of town. A couple in the midst of a nasty divorce were fighting over a pet custody issue.

But he shouldn't have been surprised. It was Memorial Day weekend. Holidays—and full moons—seemed to bring out the worst in people.

He'd spent the better part of the week trying to resolve the domestic conflict. And right now, his on-duty officers were tied up with a multiple-vehicle collision on one of the main traffic arteries outside town.

Because he'd established a measure of trust with the parties involved, he knew he needed to respond to this one himself. Speed-dialing Maggie, he explained his dilemma.

"I'm so sorry to bother you. After you've spent the entire week taking care of them, you deserve your weekend off. And I wouldn't ask if it wasn't—"

"No problem. Small-town police department. Trust me, I completely understand. I'm a police chief's daughter, remember? We'll have a great time."

She sounded elated at the prospect of having the boys over to her house. No question about it. Maggie was a treasure. With his mom in Fayetteville, he didn't know how he would've managed without her.

After dropping the twins off, he hurried away to intervene before the war of words escalated into something irreversible. Eventually, he was able to defuse the situation—for now—but it meant he was late arriving at the Memorial Day weekend ice-cream social.

Over dinner last night, Tom Arledge had invited him to attend the church get-together at the Apple Valley Orchard.

It sounded like fun. The ice cream was an added bonus. And a more relaxed way to connect with other believers. He was eager to put down real roots—physical and spiritual—in the Truelove community. But leaving the scene, he realized he'd never make it on time, so he texted Maggie he was running late.

His phone beeped with an incoming message. Dad, boys and I will meet u @ party. M

He pulled up to his house and stepped out of the cruiser. The typed *M* in the text made him smile.

She'd started leaving colorful, handwritten sticky notes on the fridge for him to find in the morning. At first, the notes contained a rundown of their schedule for the day. Then other notes posed questions about food preferences for dinner. Lately, the notes had evolved into silly smiley faces and wishing him a great day.

At the bottom of the notes, she signed only her first initial. An *M* with an artistic flourish. The notes had become the highlight of his day.

Maggie was devoted to the twins. He couldn't fault her for that. They were happy. Well fed. Well looked after. The house was spotless. One of the many things not in her job description she did without hesitation. As if she was determined to make herself indispensable.

So why couldn't he shake the feeling there was something he was missing?

After a quick shower, he shrugged on the blue shirt his sister had given him for Christmas last year. Calling the shirt dressy casual, Shannon said it matched his eyes.

His taste in clothes leaned toward the more comfortable side. This was the first time he'd actually had occasion to wear it.

A no-fuss, no-muss kind of guy, after donning a pair of jeans and running a comb through his hair, he was out the door again in less than ten minutes.

Tom had texted him the address to the orchard. It didn't take long to reach the farm. He drove the truck under the crossbars.

Bypassing a rustic country store, he continued on the long gravel-covered drive lined with leafed-out apple trees. Set on a knoll overlooking the orchard, the white two-story farmhouse had a tin roof that gleamed in the late-afternoon sun. A bevy of vehicles were parked off to the side.

Stepping out, he heard the sound of children's voices coming from the backyard. Rounding the corner of the house, he found the backyard bustling with activity. Ice-cream churns sat atop tables outside the barn. Without meaning to, he searched the crowd for Maggie and the twins.

Amid an informal grouping of lawn chairs, a small cluster of people chatted under the shade of a dogwood. Maggie sat between her aunt GeorgeAnne and the other two matchmakers. The twins played in a nearby sand-box.

Catching sight of him at the same instant he spotted her, Maggie waved him over. Her smile caused the bottom to drop out of his stomach. Stuffing his hands in his jean pockets, he strolled over to the boys first. Austin called a cheerful hello. Logan ignored him. He moved on to the adults.

Sipping lemonade, GeorgeAnne leaned back in an Adirondack chair. "Chief."

"Miss GeorgeAnne." He dipped his chin to acknowledge the other two ladies. "Miss ErmaJean. Miss Ida-Lee."

Then, unable to resist the visual feast that was Maggie any longer, he swung his gaze in her direction. She was stunning in white jeans and a turquoise blouse.

Even though she lived in yoga pants and exercise clothes, she always looked good to him. But seeing her dressed up for the occasion was spectacular.

"Glad to see you made it, son." Her father clapped

a hand on his shoulder, jerking his attention off Maggie. "You've met Nash Jackson." Tom pointed toward a fiftysomething couple manning the ice-cream churns. "And that's his wife, Lorena."

"They live here, right?"

"Nash used to." GeorgeAnne cocked her head. "Till he came to his senses and married Lorena."

A tall man with dark blond hair laughed. He stood behind what Bridger took to be his very pregnant wife, seated in one of the chairs.

"I'm Jake McAbee, Chief Hollingsworth. Nash's son-in-law." He rested his hand on his wife's shoulder. "Thanks to the matchmakers, he wasn't the only one to come to his senses."

GeorgeAnne threw the young man a fond smile. "We do what we can."

He wasn't touching that with a ten-foot pole. "Pleased to meet you, Jake. Call me Bridger."

"I'm Callie." Reaching up, Jake's wife caught her husband's hand, twining her fingers through his. "Now my father lives down the road, but he and Jake still run the orchard together."

Her gesture was so unconscious and sweet, something caught in Bridger's chest. Again, without meaning to, his eyes flicked toward Maggie.

More introductions followed. This was his first so-called social outing. He was surprised at the number of couples his age. And as each laughingly recalled, one or all the matchmakers had a hand in their happily-ever-afters.

From the look of things, Amber Green was another good friend of Maggie's. She and her husband, Ethan, had twins like him. He smiled to himself.

He made a note to get to know Ethan better. Lucy and Stella were blonde dynamos in perpetual motion. Their father could be a fount of wisdom for a newbie twin parent like himself.

A cowboy introduced himself and his wife, a vivacious redhead. Their little son was a mini-me of his father.

He scrunched his forehead, concentrating on committing their names to memory, too. AnnaBeth and Jonas Stone. Their son's name was...

Maggie nudged him with her shoulder. "I'll make you a list."

He scrubbed his face. "That would be most appreciated. 'Cause if I understand correctly, Amber's dad, Dwight, is married to Jonas's mom, Deirdre?"

She laughed. "The matchmakers at their finest."

His jaw dropped. "For real?"

"Yep." She smirked. "Aunt G and the ladies like to stay busy. No unattached person from any generation is safe from their reach." She patted his shoulder. "They'll probably have you matrimonially hog-tied before Thanksgiving."

"They can try." He snorted, letting her see him take a good look at her bare hand. "But not you?"

"No. Not me." Gaze dropping, she stepped back. "I think I'll try Deirdre's famous blackberry ice cream now. Can I get you something?" Before he could respond, though, she moved away.

Leaning against one of the oaks, he watched her chatting with her friends. Her manner relaxed and easy. Her smile back in place.

Maggie was a mystery. And the thing was he loved nothing so much as putting together the pieces of a puzzle. The challenge of a mystery to solve. It was why he'd made a good detective.

He sensed there were a lot of layers beneath the cheerful, energetic fitness trainer persona she presented to the world. She was an interesting woman with hidden depths. She intrigued him.

Somewhere along the way, his reasoning behind the desire to know her better had gotten blurred. For the sake of the twins? Or was he thinking of himself, too?

After everyone had their fill of ice cream, Jake offered each child a ride on his green tractor.

Maggie took lots of photos of the twins sitting in Jake's lap. Logan's face, so serious, was a picture of concentration. Bridger chuckled.

His little hands gripping the wheel, Logan probably believed he was single-handedly driving the tractor through the rows of apple trees by himself. When it was daredevil Austin's turn, Jake wisely kept a secure hold around his waist to prevent any mishaps.

Later, Jake hooked up the wagon used for hayrides during apple-harvest season. Since Bridger was helping himself to another bowl of peach ice cream—okay, his third—Tom offered to ride in his place and supervise the twins.

The tractor and hay wagon disappeared over the hill. Seconds later, the door off the screened porch creaked. Skipping lightly down the steps, Maggie appeared with a wet dishcloth in her hand. She and the older women had gone into the house to wash the churns.

"Oh." Seeing only him in the yard, she teetered to a stop. "Where is everyone?"

He pointed his spoon toward the orchard grove. "No one left but me."

She cast a hard look over her shoulder to the house. "I should've seen that one coming."

His eyebrows hitched. "Pardon?"

She frowned. "Aunt G and the ladies sent me out to wipe off the tables."

He scratched his head. "And?"

"It appears we're on their radar now." Bending, she scrubbed the table furiously. "In all likelihood, they're watching out the kitchen window."

"Gotcha."

Using her forearm, she swiped a strand of hair out of her face. "They think they're so clever sending me out here so we can be alone to talk."

He laughed.

"It's not funny." She rolled her eyes. "You don't know them like I do. Once they get an idea in their heads, they're like a dog with a bone."

"As persistent as a mosquito?"

She made a face. "And as annoying."

"Here." He held out his hand for the cloth. "Let me."

"Thanks."

Reaching behind her head, she tightened her ponytail.

Bridger's heart jackhammered. He focused on wiping down the tables. Rather than fixating on wondering what her hair would feel like in his fingers.

Have you lost your mind? Earlier today, you were convinced she was hiding something.

Yet being near her like this, his doubts had a way of melting as fast as the ice cream on this warm late-May afternoon.

Leaving the cloth on one of the tables, he plopped into a nearby lawn chair. "So since we're out here, maybe we should give 'em what they want."

She tilted her head. "Talk, you mean?"

He rested his hands on the armrests. "Maybe then they'll move on to badger somebody else."

She sat down in the chair beside him. "Good theory. No harm in trying, I guess."

And because he'd been wondering, he said what was on his mind. "I'm surprised they haven't already matched a hometown girl like yourself with someone."

Leaning back, she closed her eyes. "I think because of before, Aunt G has kept me out of their schemes."

"A previous relationship that ended badly?"

Her eyes flew open. "Something like that."

"Something we have in common." He grimaced. "How long ago?"

Dropping her gaze, she smoothed a fold in her jeans. "Three years."

"So painful you've not jumped back into the dating pool since, huh?"

A vein in the hollow of her throat throbbed. "Yes."

"Believe me, I get where you're coming from."

She studied him for a long moment.

Would she open up to him? Despite daily contact, he felt like he barely knew her. Would she talk to him about her life? It surprised him how much he wanted to know her. All about her.

"I was never good at the whole dating thing anyway." She fiddled with the silver chain dangling from her neck. "I was a tomboy. Preferred to be outdoors. Played high school sports. Got a volleyball scholarship to college."

He released the tiny breath he hadn't realized he was holding. They did have a lot in common. She was athletic. Same as him, except his sport in high school and college had been football.

Other than the silver knot earrings she wore every day, he realized she didn't usually wear jewelry. Or, makeup. Not that she needed it in his opinion. He preferred her girl-next-door, freshly scrubbed look.

She jiggled her knee. As if she were jittery. "How long ago did you break up with your girlfriend?"

Had she been working up the courage to ask him that?

Bridger caught himself at odd moments of the day thinking about her. Wondering about what she was doing. Had she wondered about him, too?

"Eight months ago." A lump settled in the base of his throat. "She was actually my fiancée."

"Oh." She moistened her lips. "High school sweethearts?"

"College."

When she didn't say anything, he looked at her. "We got engaged after I finished the police academy."

She still didn't say anything.

"Chelsea was one of those women who believe they must always have a man in their life. Their lives revolve around their boyfriends so much that without them, they have no identity of their own."

Maggie's brow creased.

Chelsea was the antithesis of strong, independent Maggie. What must she think of him, getting involved with a woman like that?

"She was needy. Clingy. Demanding. In hysterics if I wasn't with her every possible moment of every day."

Maggie fingered her earring. "That must have been… exhausting."

"It was." He blew out a breath. "She was this bright, bubbly, social butterfly on the surface. But inside, she was a black hole of insecurity. She pretty much went to pieces every time I went on an undercover assignment. And I could be gone for weeks at a time."

"Law enforcement is tough for significant others and spouses. Dealing with the stress of not knowing if your loved one will ever come home again."

He stretched out his legs. "But your mom coped?"

Maggie nodded. "I think it requires a particular kind of personality to handle the uncertainty. How about your mom, Wilda?"

"She was, and continues to be, the rock of the Hollingsworth family."

The more he got to know Maggie, the more she reminded him of his mother. Maggie would probably make a good law enforcement wife.

She inched forward in her chair. "I'm sorry things didn't work out with your fiancée."

Funny, because from where he was sitting, suddenly he wasn't sorry at all.

"Like I said, when I was away on assignment, Chelsea didn't cope too well. So she found…other ways to occupy herself." He raised his lip. "With a spare boyfriend on the side."

Her eyes shot to his. "Oh, Bridger."

"Turns out, their relationship started years earlier while I was at the academy." He grunted. "I finished an assignment one day sooner than expected, and I found them together."

Maggie's face gentled. "That must have been so painful."

"Try *humiliating*. She totally played me. Lied over and over again to my face." He slumped. "Like a chump, I fell for it, every single time. My family proved a better judge of character than me. They never liked her. Not even back in college."

Maggie's mouth pulled downward. "And since then, you've had a hard time trusting people."

He tightened his jaw. "Trusting myself, too."

Maggie knotted her hands in her lap. "I know how demoralizing it is to doubt yourself."

"She betrayed me. Chelsea was the biggest mistake of my life," he growled. "A mistake I don't intend to repeat. You know what they say about the burned child."

Maggie sighed. "They dread the fire."

"I should've never gotten involved with her. But I wasn't a Christian then."

"Wait." Maggie sat up. "You discovered your fiancée cheating on you eight months ago. And your brother was killed four months later?"

"Yeah." He combed his fingers through the short ends of his hair. "It's been a rough year. Yet the situation with Chelsea and my brother's death drove me to my knees. I realized I had no hope of doing life—much less raising the twins—without His help."

She faced forward. "I'd drifted away from God during college, too. But after what happened—"

"After you broke up with your boyfriend?"

"He's n—" She pressed her lips together. "Anyway, I came home to Truelove and my faith."

So that was why she'd left Atlanta. A relationship gone sour. Or worse?

Recalling the stark fear he'd glimpsed in her eyes when he accidentally touched her that once, a sudden, sick suspicion twisted his gut.

Bridger searched her features. Had her jerk boyfriend been abusive? Hit her? Beaten her? It would explain so much.

No wonder she was so easily startled. No wonder she had a hard time trusting men. Did her father know? Did anyone in Truelove know?

Had she actually shared something so painfully personal just with him? How alone she must have felt.

Bridger knew what it felt like to be trapped in a toxic relationship. He had nothing but contempt for men who were physically or emotionally violent toward women. And he'd seen far too many cases of domestic abuse in his career to not have a clear picture of what Maggie had been through.

Heart thundering, blood pounded in his ears. If he ever got his hands on the man who'd dared lay hands on her... He might forget he was supposed to uphold the law, not resort to vigilante justice.

"Bridger? What is it?" She laid her hand on top of his.

A shiver went through him.

"You're safe with me, Maggie." His fist slowly uncurled. "I want you to know I'd never hurt you. Or allow anyone to ever hurt you again," he rasped.

She looked at him strangely. "From the first, I think I sensed that about you," she whispered.

They sat there hand in hand for another minute until the tractor chugged over the hill. Jumping to her feet, she scooped up the dishcloth and headed toward the house, leaving him staring after her.

Amid the joyful commotion of everyone disembarking from the hay wagon, he believed he heard another sound, as well.

The sound of another barrier falling from his heart.

Chapter Seven

Almost a week after the ice-cream social, on Friday morning Bridger surprised Maggie when he came into the kitchen carrying a small duffel bag.

"Last year, I was the arresting officer in a drug sting. The assistant DA contacted me last night. The state's case against the drug dealer got moved up on the court's docket. The prosecutor needs me to testify today."

Sunlight streamed through the window over the sink. She loved this time of day the best. "Okay." She poured herself a cup of coffee.

He frowned. "In Raleigh."

Nodding, she took a sip of coffee.

He placed his duffel on the floor. "Raleigh is four and a half hours away. I'll be gone all day."

She knew the distance to Raleigh. What was his point? 'Cause she was getting the sense he had one.

When she didn't reply, his gaze narrowed. "Will you be okay here with the boys?"

Getting annoyed, she lowered the cup. "Why wouldn't the boys and I be okay?"

At the ice-cream social, she'd believed he'd finally

begun to lower his guard with her. When he shared his feelings of raw vulnerability, she'd been moved beyond words. So moved she'd reached for his hand. Shocking herself.

She'd spent far too many moments reliving the feel of his hand. His calloused palm, warm and strong.

But it was like he was embarrassed to have opened up to her. As if she would think less of him for his fiancée's betrayal. Ever since, he'd kept her at arm's length. All business. All the time.

"I'm scheduled to testify before noon, but if the defense's cross-examination runs late, the judge could require me to return to the stand tomorrow."

From the twins' bedroom, she heard the sound of drawers closing. Probably dressing themselves. A situation she'd need to sort, and soon.

He scrubbed his chin. "Would you be able to stay with the boys overnight if I'm unable to get away? Or will that be a problem?"

"I'm happy to stay with the boys overnight." She tilted her head. "Why would there be a problem?"

He rubbed the back of his neck. "Perhaps you had plans for tonight." His face reddened and his gaze dropped to his feet. "I didn't want to presume."

Was this weird interrogation about her dependability, or more of a fishing expedition regarding her availability? As in single-status availability?

Don't be an idiot. She must be delusional. Bridger wasn't interested in her. Since Memorial Day weekend, he'd barely spoken to her.

"No plans." She set the cup on the counter. "No problem."

With his head poking through the opening of his

shirt, Logan trotted into the kitchen. But in pulling it down his torso, he'd somehow managed to trap his arms against his sides like a straitjacket.

She and Bridger moved forward to help him.

"You might be unable to reach me." Bridger tugged one of Logan's arms free. "You're sure you and the boys will be all right?"

"Of course." She helped Logan insert his other arm through the sleeve. "We'll be fine."

Bridger picked up his bag. Yet, as if rooted to the floor, he didn't move. Looking ridiculously handsome. Hesitating. Waiting, but for what?

An image of a perfect morning rose in her mind. Conversation over coffee. Austin and Logan laughing at the breakfast table. Their uncle standing right where he was now. Waiting for her to give him a have-a-good-day, can't-wait-till-I-see-you kiss. A proper send-off.

Where had that come from?

Completely discombobulated by the direction of her thoughts, she lowered her gaze. "I'm not teaching today. We're planning on sticking close to home."

Still, he lingered. "I hope to see you tonight." He turned the hat in his hands. "Have a good day."

"You, too," she called in an attempt at nonchalance.

He said his goodbyes to the twins. And then he was gone.

The rest of the morning passed slowly. It had become a nice habit when they were in town to meet Bridger for lunch. If the weather was fine, they picnicked. If not, he insisted on treating them at the Jar.

It was during lunch at the house she first noticed something amiss with Austin. He refused to touch his grilled cheese sandwich, his personal favorite. When bottomless pits wouldn't eat, that was a bad sign, right? And he pitched the mother of all fits when it was time to lie down on his bed for rest time.

"What's wrong, Austin? Tell Maggie what's wrong?"

On an intellectual level, she'd known no child was always well behaved. On an emotional level, she'd not been prepared for her sunny, laid-back boy turning into a cranky, toy-throwing brat without warning. Her terrific two-year-old had suddenly morphed into a terrifying two-year-old.

"No go sweep," Austin roared. "Me no want, Magwee. Me want Nana."

She flinched.

Of course they'd want their grandmother. Maggie wasn't sure how much they recalled of their lives before the shooting. But at their age, six months constituted a fourth of their lives. Did they remember their mother, Dana? They never asked for her.

Memories or not, though, they knew Wilda. She had been their lifeline since their parents were killed. From the beginning, Maggie felt an unexplainable bond with the boys, but they'd known her only a few weeks. Maybe the feelings were on her side only.

Although hurtful to acknowledge, Austin and Logan had no reason to think of her as their mother. She was nothing more to them than the lady who took care of them while their grandmother was away.

Maggie was the reader of stories. The giver of hugs and kisses. She fed them. Gave them baths. Made them pick up their toys.

But their mother? No. That was a secret that she kept hidden deep inside her heart.

Austin's wails reverberated off the walls. From his

own bed, Logan stared at his twin like he'd never seen him before. She tried to remember everything she'd read about how to deal with toddler tantrums.

She sat with him until he calmed down. Austin fell into an exhausted sleep. Completely wrecked, she retreated to the living room. Sinking onto the couch, she put her head in her hands. What was she doing? She had no business being anyone's mother.

Unable to settle, she worked out her restlessness by scouring the sink. All remained quiet for the next thirty minutes until she heard the creak of the bedroom door.

Holding on to his teddy bear, Logan padded into the living room. "Wostin cry, Magwee."

She dashed down the hall to find Austin huddled on his bed, sobbing. Logan patted his leg. "No cry, Wostin. Magwee here."

"Austin, baby." She sank onto the mattress. "What's wrong? Is it your tummy?" She felt his forehead. "Is it your head?"

He tugged at his right ear. "Hurt, Magwee. Hurt." Opening his arms, he reached for her.

She gathered him close. "Your ear hurts, sweetheart?"

Head bobbing, he burst into fresh tears. She called Amber, a nurse who worked at the local pediatrician's office.

Recognizing the panic in Maggie's voice, Amber told her to bring Austin to the office, and she'd make sure the doctor saw him right away.

With Austin sobbing uncontrollably and Logan clinging, it was no small feat getting the boys into the car. The ride to town had never felt so long.

At the pediatrician's, Amber took care of them.

"Don't worry about the paperwork," she said, putting them in the examination room. "I'll take care of everything for you."

Amber also managed to entice Logan into staying with her in the reception area to watch the turtles in the huge aquarium tank.

The entire time the doctor checked his mouth, nose and ears, Austin maintained his stranglehold around Maggie's neck. The doctor recommended acetaminophen and ear drops for the pain.

She shifted Austin to a more comfortable position on her hip. "What about an antibiotic?"

"Most ear infections run their course on their own." The doctor rehung the stethoscope around his neck. "If he's not better in two or three days, we'll take another look and talk about antibiotics."

Two or three days? She glared at the doctor. Was he out of his mind? Her baby was in pain.

Before she could go all Mama Bear on him, however, Amber and Logan appeared in the doorway. Logan had a grape lollipop in his mouth.

"If he takes a turn for the worse, give us a call. Any hour of the day or night." The doctor patted her shoulder. "But rest assured, Mrs. Hollingsworth, your little man is going to feel better very soon."

Mrs. Hollingsworth?

Face burning, she dared not look at Amber. Maggie had never had a reason to venture into the pediatrician's office. They'd never met before. And with the chart labeled Austin Hollingsworth, the doctor assumed she was his mother.

Eyes closing, Austin settled his head into the hollow of her shoulder.

The doctor ushered her toward the checkout desk. "Nice to meet you. I'm happy you and your husband, Chief Hollingsworth, chose our practice to care for your family."

Amber bit her lip. Maggie felt like sinking into the carpet. She might be Austin's mother, but she was most definitely *not* Bridger Hollingsworth's wife.

She took a breath. "I'm not—"

"Next patient's waiting in room four, Doctor." Amber hustled her toward the lobby. "Logan picked out a lollipop for Austin when he's feeling better."

Maggie shot a glance over her shoulder at the doctor's retreating white coat. "But —"

"Let's not confuse him. Maybe next time you have to bring the boys in, you *will* be Mrs. Hollingsworth."

"Not you, too, Amber." She ground to a halt in front of the aquarium. "Don't tell me Aunt G and the matchmakers have turned you to the dark side."

"Poor little guy." Amber stroked Austin's blond curls. She flicked a too-innocent glance at Maggie. "If you can't beat 'em…" She shrugged.

"Bridger's not…" Maggie sputtered. "I'm not…"

Amber folded her arms across her lavender-blue scrubs. "What's stopping you two?"

If she only knew.

Maggie's chin quivered. The little boy in her arms and his twin stood between her and Bridger ever becoming anything more than friends.

Of even greater significance, however, was the truth she'd failed to disclose. Her relationship with Bridger was far more complicated than Amber or anyone else had any way of guessing.

Amber gave her a sample bottle of ear drops. Maggie knew the medicine cabinet at the farmhouse already contained acetaminophen.

Once she got the boys home, she texted Bridger that she'd taken Austin to the doctor. She had no way of knowing if, or when, he'd get the message. Holding Austin in her arms, she wondered if he'd be angry with her for overstepping. Although what parent would begrudge her seeking medical help?

"Me tired, Magwee," Logan whined. "Me feel bad."

She checked his forehead for fever. Surely he didn't have an ear infection, too?

When her cell phone buzzed, both twins burst into tears. And she felt like joining them.

That afternoon, Bridger emerged from the courthouse in Raleigh. Surprisingly, the prosecutor had wrapped up his testimony soon after court went back into session after lunch.

Faced with overwhelming evidence of his client's guilt, the defense attorney had declined to cross-examine. With Bridger's services no longer required, the judge released him as a witness. He was free to head home to Truelove.

He glanced at his watch. If he got on the road now, he'd likely beat rush-hour traffic. And barring any accidents or road construction, he stood a good chance of making it home in time for dinner.

A late dinner, but the idea of one of Maggie's home-cooked meals held more than a little appeal. One of the many unforeseen perks of hiring the pretty brunette. He frowned, irritated at himself.

Her abusive experience with her previous boyfriend explained a lot about her reticence. Yet there was something else about her that didn't add up. Something elusive he couldn't quite put his finger on. And he was a man who liked to be in possession of all the facts.

Maggie was great with the boys. She'd been great with the boys *so far*. Retracing his steps to the parking garage where he'd left the cruiser, he grimaced. So far?

Since his relationship debacle with Chelsea, he had a hard time not feeling as if he were waiting for the other shoe to drop. And as much as he enjoyed Maggie's company, he still felt like there was something not quite right.

He'd learned to trust his gut. And his gut was cautioning him not to let down his guard with her. Or was his bad experience with Chelsea messing with his head?

Everyone had a right to privacy. Maybe Maggie was just reserved in nature. He wasn't exactly Mr. Transparency, either. His stomach rumbled again.

But no matter how much he enjoyed her food. Or gazing into her chocolate-brown eyes. If she was hiding something, he wouldn't rest until he discovered what it was. He had the twins' welfare to consider.

Getting into the cruiser, he switched on his phone and discovered the text message she sent two hours ago. She'd taken Austin to the pediatrician. His chest squeezed. Was he sick? Had there been an accident?

He speed-dialed her cell phone. But it rang and rang until finally going to voice mail. He glared at the phone in his hand.

Where was she? Why wasn't she answering her phone? What was happening to his boys?

Teeth clenched, he brought the engine to life. Frustrated, he tore out of the parking lot. Caught in road construction, he fumed at the delay. Once out of the city, he exited onto the interstate and accelerated to make up for lost time.

It was early evening by the time he reached the outskirts of Truelove. As he pulled into the driveway, his heart leaped at the sight of not only Maggie's car, but her father's truck, too.

He jerked the cruiser to a standstill. Leaping out of the vehicle, he raced for the house. Tom met him at the door.

"Didn't get the text till..." His chest panted. "Austin... Logan..."

"Slow down, Chief." Carrying the dark-haired twin on his hip, Tom ushered him inside. "Logan and I have been reading books."

He rushed past them. "What happened? What're you doing here? Where's—" He came to a standstill.

Eyes closed, Maggie lay stretched out on the sofa. With her arms wrapped around the conked-out little boy, Austin's cheek lay pressed against her shirt.

Tom put his finger to his lips. "So far so good with Logan. He appears to be feeling well, at least for now. Austin is completely tuckered out but fine," he whispered. "It's been a rough afternoon. She finally got him to sleep and fell asleep herself."

He gulped. "What's wrong with Austin?"

"Ear infection. Painful, but no cause for panic. Maggie used to get those when she was a little girl." He squeezed Bridger's shoulder. "I happened to call right after she got back from the doctor. I volunteered to entertain Logan so she could concentrate on Austin." Tom winked at the little boy. "We've had a good time, haven't we, sport?"

Logan put his chubby finger to his mouth. "Shhhhh… Wostin sick."

Nearly sick with relief, Bridger touched his hand to the child's straight dark hair. And for once, Logan didn't shy away.

As a cop, he was predisposed to expecting tragedy around every corner. So often he'd been involved in what was the worst day of people's lives. Time to stop allowing his relationship with Chelsea to color how he viewed the world.

Bridger forced a trickle of breath into his tight lungs. Not a good way to live. He had two young boys depending on him to teach them emotional and spiritual health.

He'd become far too skilled at holding back his true self. Keeping others at arm's length. If he wanted to be a good parent, being emotionally unavailable wasn't going to cut it.

I need to do better, God. Help me to trust You. To open myself to the fear, the hurt and the pain that comes from loving others.

Gaining control of his rapidly beating heart, he inched toward the couch.

Seeing Maggie cuddle the small boy in her arms made a strange feeling rustle in his chest. Another image flashed through his brain. Of Maggie, surrounded by Austin and Logan, her belly large with his child.

A picture so sharply sweet, it momentarily robbed him of breath and set him back on his heels.

What was with him? She was the twins' caregiver. Anything else was not only inappropriate but a recipe for disaster.

Crouching alongside the sofa, he touched Austin's arm. "Sorry you're sick."

The child's eyes flew open. Letting go of Maggie, Austin reached for him. "Bwidge. Bwidge."

As he scrambled over Maggie, his knee pressed into her stomach. Air whooshed from her lungs. Her eyes flew open. Bleary-eyed, she pushed her hair out of her face where it had come undone from the usual pony-tail. When her gaze landed on him, she bolted upright.

Alarm streaked across her features. "I—I'm sorry. I don't normally fall asleep when I'm with the twins."

Did he really come off so unbending that she was afraid of him? Why did she get so agitated around him? Was he that intimidating and threatening?

"Your father explained everything." Regret flickered through him. "I'm sorry you couldn't get ahold of me, and had to deal with this on your own."

Getting off the couch, she extended her arms to Logan. Without a second thought, he left Tom and went to her. Rubbing little circles on his back, she hugged the child close.

"Thank you, Maggie." Settling Austin in the crook of his arm, Bridger lumbered to his feet. "I'm not sure I would've coped as well if I'd been on my own when he got sick."

"I wouldn't have wanted to be anywhere but with Austin when he was feeling bad." Her eyes probed his. "If something ever happens when you're with them, you can call me, day or night, and I'll come."

Suddenly, the doubts he'd harbored seemed base-less. He could count on Maggie to care for his boys as if they were her own.

He was ashamed of ever doubting her. She was to-tally trustworthy. Maybe more so than any other woman he'd ever known.

Instead of questioning her motives, perhaps it was time he concentrated on proving himself trustworthy to her.

Over the next few days, it seemed to Maggie that the cloud that had overshadowed Bridger appeared to have lifted.

She was supposed to have the weekend off, but she couldn't bear to be away from her sick little boy. She wanted to be near in case he needed her. Therefore, she and Bridger spent a lot of time together that weekend.

And something shifted between them.

Bridger smiled more—at her. He appeared more relaxed in her company. He laughed more often.

He spent a great deal of time entertaining the little patient. Logan didn't join in their play, but when Austin would tire of one game, it was Logan who handed Bridger another one. Bridger was settling into his new role of fatherhood.

Logan remained earache-free. Austin made a full recovery over the next two days. By Monday, he'd bounced back to his usual, energetic self.

That afternoon, she was taking stock of the emptiness of the Hollingsworth cupboards when she heard the police cruiser pull into the driveway.

She was pathetic. She knew the sound of his engine. And the sound of his truck, too.

The back door creaked as Bridger popped his head around the doorframe.

She couldn't help the rush of gladness at seeing him. "You're home early."

He leaned the long length of himself against the doorjamb. "Decided to take some time for myself and the boys. Trying to relearn bad habits. New Year's res-olution."

She closed the cabinet door. "It's June, not January."

He gave her a funny smile. "Somehow it feels like a new start for me."

"What's this bad habit you're trying to relearn?"

"As police chief, it's easy to begin to believe it's all about me. Nothing more than ego, though. I have a good team. So I can take the time every once and again to enjoy a couple of two-year-olds."

She was pleased that, at this early stage in his career, he understood the value of time with family.

"Of course, I'm not adverse to spending more time with their beautiful sitter, either."

She blushed. She wasn't beautiful by any stretch of the imagination. But somehow when she was with him, she felt beautiful.

He straightened. "But there I go presuming again. You worked well beyond the call of duty over the week-end. You deserve time off from us, too." He shuffled his feet. "Maybe there's someone else you'd like to spend time with?"

She looked at him. *Definitely fishing this time.* Beneath the stubble, his cheeks had darkened with color, but his eyes never left hers.

"There's no one else I'd rather be with, Bridger," she rasped.

He squared his shoulders. "Good."

"Actually…" She bit her lip. "I was thinking it was time for a trip to the grocery store."

"Oh." He slumped. "Sure. If you make me a list, the boys and I—"

"Friends don't let friends take twins grocery shopping alone."

He cocked his head. "That bad, huh?"

"Said by someone who's never taken twins to the grocery store."

He laughed. "Now who's presuming?"

She planted her hands on her hips. "Did your mother leave the pantry fully stocked before she left or not?"

He smirked. "She did."

"Then I rest my case."

"So what I'm hearing is you're offering to go with me into town and guide me through the food-buying ropes."

Maggie shook her head. "You're way beyond the little store in Truelove, Chief Hollingsworth. I'm afraid there's nothing for it but a trip to the big supermarket at the county seat."

The boys were thrilled to go on an outing in the middle of the day. Thirty minutes later, Bridger parked his truck outside the large supermarket. Once inside, the twins debated whether to ride in the spaceship or the dinosaur kid cart. They chose the spaceship.

Bridger scratched his head. "Who knew grocery shopping could be so complicated?"

Maggie took hold of the kid cart. "You push the regular cart. And you haven't seen the half of it yet, my friend."

Strolling the aisles was fun. Strapped into their spaceship, the boys were content to sit back and take in the view.

Bridger grinned. "That's the life."

She smiled. "A good gig if you can get it."

Perusing the shelves together, he loaded items from her list into the cart.

"Daddy, wook!" Straining against the straps, Austin pointed to a high shelf. "Me wike dat cereal."

Logan beat his heels against the footrest. "Me wike, too, Daddy."

Bridger froze. Frowning, he turned away so she could no longer see his face. She didn't like not being able to see his face.

She cleared her throat. "Sorry, guys. But I have three rules about cereal, and that one doesn't make the cut."

Bridger snapped his head around. "You have rules about cereal?" he grunted.

She raised her index finger. "I do not buy cereal that has chocolate in it." She ticked off a second finger. "I do not buy cereal with different colors."

His mouth twitched. "I can't wait to hear number three."

She held up three fingers. "No added sugar."

Logan hung his head. "Awww…"

A spark of humor glinted in Bridger's eyes. "Killjoy."

She fluttered her lashes at him. "Trust me. Their teeth and your bank account will thank me someday."

Austin pushed out his lips. "But, Daddy—"

Bridger's smile faded. "Are we about done here?"

She nodded.

Having an extra pair of hands made going through checkout seem like a walk in the park.

"What cute little boys," the teenage cashier cooed. "Are they twins?"

Bridger brushed his hand over Austin's blond head. "They are."

The teenager handed him the receipt. "You two have a beautiful family."

He winked at Maggie. "Thank you."

She gave him a look, which he ignored.

The girl continued chatting. "The one with dark hair looks just like his mother."

Fear burbled in her throat. And her gaze darted to Bridger. But, still smiling, he steered the cart toward the sliding glass doors.

Unbuckling the boys from the spaceship, she hid her flaming face. Then taking each boy firmly by the hand, she followed him out to the parking lot.

By the time she had the twins secured in their car seats, he had the groceries stowed. In a few minutes, he pulled out onto the freeway to return to Truelove. It didn't take long for the boys to fall asleep in the back seat. They'd missed their nap.

She decided to tackle the issue she'd spent much of the weekend pondering. It was getting harder to justify her doubts about his parenting ability. "Don't you think it's time to let them call you Daddy?"

He scowled. "Jeff is their father."

"They need to call someone Daddy. No offense to your brother. Jeff was a great guy."

Forehead creasing, he cut his eyes to her.

"A-at least, from what I've heard about him," she stammered.

He nodded.

"But they won't remember Jeff." She opened her palms. "You're the only father they're ever going to know."

His hands fisted the wheel. "I guess… I don't feel worthy."

"God brought the twins into your life for a reason, Bridger. He'll make you into the father Austin and Logan need."

He smiled, tiny lines fanning out from the corners of his eyes. "Thank you, Maggie. Your faith in me means more than you know."

Every day, his connection to the boys grew stronger. And their connection to him. Which was as it should be. Natural and right. Exactly what Dana and Jeff had wanted. She should've been happy. Thrilled.

And she was… Sort of.

But Bridger's growing bond with the twins left her with lots of nagging questions.

Where did she fit into their lives? Did the twins really need her anymore? In helping Bridger and her sons connect, had she also succeeded in making herself obsolete?

Chapter Eight

Thursday evening, Maggie taught the Baby Mama class at the rec center.

Designed specifically for mothers-to-be, the class combined prenatal Pilates stretching and core strength training. Her goal was to improve their cardiovascular health with the added bonus of building their stamina for labor, delivery and recovery after childbirth.

She'd battled anxiety and depression during her own difficult pregnancy. If only then she'd known about the benefits of stress-relieving exercises.

After ending the class, she walked Callie out to the parking lot. "Before long, you'll be holding your little one in your arms. It'll be worth all the aches and pains."

Callie stopped on the sidewalk. "I can't see my feet anymore, Mags. I feel so huge." She shook her head. "I certainly don't look like the girl Jake married."

Her stomach distended with twins, Maggie knew firsthand what huge really looked like. The last trimester she'd resembled a bloated whale.

Spotting Callie's husband in his truck, Maggie

waved. "You look beautiful. And I'm sure Jake thinks so, too."

"You probably think I'm being r-ridiculous." Callie's voice hitched.

She sympathized, but she couldn't tell Callie how well she understood. "I think it's normal to feel overwhelmed by the changes happening to your body."

Yet it was hard not to envy Callie.

Callie was so in love with her adoring husband. A situation as different from Maggie's pregnancy as night from day. It made her sad to think she'd never know what that was like. Something must have shown on her face because Callie took hold of her arm.

"We lost touch when you went off to college, but I can't tell you how much your friendship has meant to me since you came back to town."

Maggie swallowed.

"People tell me I'm a pretty good listener, and if you ever need to confide in someone…" Callie's gaze bored into hers. "I'm here for you."

Maggie's eyes swam. One of the best decisions she ever made had been coming home. Yet how could she even begin to share what had happened to her with Callie? She still wasn't sure she understood it herself.

Over time, the nightmares and post-traumatic stress disorder from the attack had faded. She knew there was healing in the telling. But she couldn't face it. Not yet. Maybe she never would. Perhaps some pain went too deep for anyone but God.

She hugged Callie. "You'll never know how much I appreciate your friendship."

Callie swiped her eyes. "You're coming to the baby shower this weekend, right?"

"Wouldn't miss it for the world."

A month ago, she wouldn't have felt the same.

Calling goodbye, Callie slipped inside the truck. Maggie headed toward her own vehicle at the end of the row. She liked to park close to the gym in a well-lit area.

Despite the long hours of summer light, tonight it had gotten dark earlier than she'd expected. Clicking her key fob, she popped her trunk and stowed her gym bag.

Opening the car door, she felt the first drops of rain splatter her arm. Lifting her gaze, she spotted dark clouds building on the distant mountain horizon.

Jake pulled the truck behind her car. Engine idling, he rolled down the window. "A storm is headed our way. Forecast is calling for torrential rain and significant wind gusts. I'll follow you to make sure you get home."

The mountain valleys were especially vulnerable to flash floods. Last year, Amber and her twins nearly drowned when a mudslide swept their car into the raging, swollen river.

Maggie shook her head. "Thanks, but I'll be fine."

He frowned. "I don't mind. That's what friends are for."

"Dad's waiting for me at home. Your little girl's waiting for you. I'll be okay. Really."

Callie leaned toward his open window. "Call me when you get home so we don't worry, Mags."

"That's not nec—"

"Stop being so stubborn." Callie wagged her finger. "Either call me, or I'll be sending my husband to look for you."

Maggie lifted her hand. "I'll call soon as I get into the driveway."

Callie gave her a thumbs-up. Jake didn't pull away

until she was safely inside her vehicle and started her car. It was one of the things she loved most about her hometown—how everybody took care of each other.

Sure, the downside was everybody also knew everybody else's business—and didn't mind sticking their noses into it. But she'd take small-town community any day over big-city indifference.

Rattling over the bridge out of town, she jumped at the crackle of lightning. And with that, sheets of rain fell from the sky. She switched on the windshield wipers, yet even at the highest speed, she was hard-pressed to see the road through the gushing downpour.

Jake stayed with her until she approached the turn-off to her house. She flashed her lights to let him know she could make it from here. As she veered onto the secondary road, his red taillights disappeared over the rise behind her.

She was almost home when she remembered Wilda's warning about how scared the twins were of thunderstorms. Worry dropped like a lead ball into the pit of her stomach. Her foot pressed the accelerator. Her heart pounded.

Bypassing her own driveway, she sped down the road toward the Hollingsworth home. Bringing the car to a rocking standstill, she clambered out and barreled to the front door. Hands shaking, she inserted the key into the lock.

Thunder boomed, echoing across the mountain ridge. She flinched. Lightning sizzled the sky. The knob turned in her hand, and she hurtled inside the house.

Like twin jack-in-the-boxes, Austin's and Logan's heads popped over the top of the couch.

"Magwee?"

"Hey, Magwee."

In their pajamas, the boys were dressed for bed.

Brows furrowed, Bridger sat up from where he and the boys had been lounging on the couch. Dripping on the hardwood floor, in her headlong rush to take care of her sons, she hadn't paused to consider what she would actually say. After barging, uninvited, into their house.

Moving the boys off his lap, Bridger got off the sofa. "Are you all right? Is something wrong?"

Dumbfounded, she blinked at him. Her gaze ping-ponged between the open book in his hand and the twins. Neither of whom appeared the least bit frightened by the storm.

Eyes wide, all three Hollingsworths appeared more alarmed by her sudden appearance than by the storm. She stared at them for a moment. Then closed her eyes. She must look like a crazed, drowned rat.

She felt Bridger move around the sofa toward her. Even with her eyes closed she was always very aware of him. Like the exact second he entered a room or exited. And always, his proximity to her. With him, it was like she had a kind of internal radar.

"Maggie?"

She opened her eyes. "I—I was worried the boys would be frightened by the storm." She gestured to the window.

He hefted the children's book in his hand. "I asked some of the cops who were dads for advice. They gave me some tips. I stopped at a bookstore when I was in Raleigh. The bookseller recommended this book."

The cover depicted every child's favorite storybook turtle. The book was a classic about overcoming a fear of storms.

She'd worried for nothing. He'd been aware of their anxiety. He'd sought advice from other dads. He'd done his homework.

"We've been reading it a couple of nights a week. I knew sooner or later, as summer progressed, a thunderstorm was bound to happen."

He'd been proactive in helping them overcome their fears. He'd done everything right. The very definition of responsible and caring parenting.

Maggie's doubts about his ability to parent the twins dissipated. For the first time since discovering the truth about her sons, she was ready to acknowledge Bridger Hollingsworth was the best possible father Dana and Jeff could've chosen for her sons.

Not her sons. Bridger's sons.

"I'm sorry," she whispered in a small voice. "I wanted to be sure they were okay. I shouldn't have…"

She was an interfering idiot. The uncomfortable truth was she needed the twins more than they needed her.

"I should go."

"Wait." He caught her elbow. "Since you're here, there's no need to go. We're always glad to see you." He threw a glance over his shoulder. "Aren't we, boys?"

"Yay! Yay! Hoo-way!"

Austin and Logan jumped on the cushions.

"Stop—"

"Don't—"

She and Bridger looked at each other.

He smiled. "Great minds…"

It was disconcerting how in sync she felt with him. "You grab one twin, and I'll grab the other?"

"Before stitches are required?" He smirked. "Sure."

They moved forward as one.

"Stop jumping..."

"...on the couch."

He grinned. She bit the inside of her cheek. Her aunt would've had a field day with their finishing each other's sentences.

It required their combined ingenuity and strength to wrestle the boys into bed for the night. Bridger asked her to stay and help the boys say their bedtime prayers. A privilege she'd never in her wildest dreams imagined would ever be hers.

More perfect than a dream, though. Because Bridger was there, too. His prayers joining hers, he rested his hand on each child's head in turn. She'd never tire of their little arms around her neck and the sweet goodnight kisses on her cheek.

She and Bridger edged toward the door. "See you in the morning." She waggled her fingers at them.

"Wuv you, Mag—" Austin yawned "—wee."

"Me wuv, wuv, wuv you, Magwee," Logan chimed, not to be outdone.

She blew them both a kiss. "I love you both so, so much."

Bridger toggled the light switch. "What about dear old Dad? Or am I nothing but a bunch of turtle poop to you guys?"

Howls of laughter erupted from the beds.

She rolled her eyes. "Thirty-one, thirteen or two, does the male species ever outgrow the love of potty humor?"

"Nope." He grinned.

She arched her brow. "You've got them riled up all over again."

"Worth it if it means you'll consider staying awhile

longer." He cupped his hand over his mouth. "Tell Maggie good-night, little gators."

"Night-night, Magwee," Austin called.

"While cwoc-o-dile," Logan said.

"Go to sleep," she told them and closed the door.

Childish giggles erupted on the other side of the door.

He exhaled. "I may be in for a long night."

She pursed her lips. "A long night of your own making."

He crossed his arms over his chest. "Sounds like the storm has blown over. Want to hang out with me awhile?" His gaze darted to hers, a shy uncertainty on his face. "Unless you need to get home."

She could think of no other place she'd rather be. "I—I'd like that."

His mouth curved. "Great."

Just then her phone buzzed in the pocket of her exercise capris. She knew without looking who was calling. She'd forgotten to text Callie and let her know she was safely home.

Digging out her cell to reassure Callie, she followed Bridger into the living room.

Technically, she wasn't at home. But somehow, it felt like for once she was both safe *and* home.

What followed was perhaps the best night of Bridger's life.

After sending her dad a text to let him know her whereabouts, Maggie stayed to talk. Removing the band on her ponytail, she shook out her wet locks and towel-dried her hair. With her hair down, she appeared somehow softer to him. And even more lovely.

Earlier in the week, she'd seemed distant with him.

Maybe since the grocery expedition. Was it just his imagination or the push-pull thing with her that left him feeling off-kilter?

He'd been surprised when she burst through the door. Surprised but pleased to see her.

They reminisced about childhood memories. He especially enjoyed hearing her talk about growing up in the little Blue Ridge town where Austin and Logan would now grow up, too.

He and the beautiful brunette had a lot in common— starting with both of them coming from law enforcement families.

They shared the stability of great parents. Happy childhoods. And the loss of one of those beloved parents.

He found himself telling her about the fun he, Jeff and Shannon had as children.

"I always wanted a brother or sister," she whispered in a wistful voice.

He told her how he'd tried to emulate his older brother his entire life. And when he looked up, he found silent tears sliding down her cheeks.

Bridger's heart leaped into his throat. "I didn't mean to make you cry."

"I'm so sorry you lost him. Especially that way."

He scrubbed his hand over his face. "It shook me. It shook us all. But losing Jeff brought me back to God. Although, at the time, I had no idea how God could bring any kind of beauty out of such tragedy, but He has."

"Beauty out of ashes." Her chin dropped. "I get where you're coming from."

He held his breath as she shared a few of her own struggles to trust God since her mother died. He sensed there was more she didn't say. And she didn't appear to have a man in her life.

Either the Truelove male population was stupid and blind, or because of leftover baggage from her last jerk boyfriend, she wasn't interested in pursuing a relationship with anyone.

After what happened with Chelsea, he could relate.

Talking about her mother, it was the first time she'd opened up to him about anything so personal. The first time she allowed him a glimpse inside her heart. Not an all-encompassing view by any means. But it was a start. Was she beginning to trust him?

He smiled. "Meeting you has been one of the beautiful things God has brought into my life."

Color bloomed on her cheeks. She gathered her hair off her shoulders into a messy bun. "It's gotten late. I should go."

He stood with her. "Text me when you get home, please?"

She nodded. "Are you busy after work tomorrow?"

He broadened his chest. "Whatever you have in mind, count me in."

She tilted her head. "You haven't heard what I was going to say."

He stuck his hands in his jeans. "Doesn't matter."

A smile crept across her lips. "It involves the twins and shoe shopping."

"Will this adventure include you?"

She looked at him. "Do you want it to include me?"

"Yes, I do."

She smiled at him then, in a way he didn't believe she'd ever smiled at him before. With her entire face. Her eyes lighting up. A dimple appearing in her cheek.

And his heart dropped like a runaway elevator in a shaft. Slamming down somewhere in the region of his toes.

"Okay, then." She wrenched open the door. "See you later, alligator."

"After a while, crocodile," he rasped, trying to recover from whatever it was Maggie Arledge had hit him with.

He'd always liked athletic women, but when she smiled like that, she knocked his socks off. If he'd been wearing socks, that is.

The next day at the station, he was a little distracted. Okay, a lot distracted. But it was a slow crime day. So no harm, no foul. And he didn't let any grass grow under his feet heading home.

He texted Maggie he was on his way. She had the boys dressed and raring to go when he pulled into the drive.

They stopped for supper at a retro-style diner on the interstate. The hostess seated them in a booth close to the entrance.

He hoisted Logan into the booster seat.

Logan caught his hand. "Me wike chocolate."

Blowing a strand of hair out of her face, Maggie strapped the bucking bronco also known as Austin Hollingsworth into his seat.

Throughout dinner, Bridger's gaze returned again and again to her smile, her expressive face, her dark chocolate eyes…

He glanced across the booth at Logan's baby face smeared with the remains of his milkshake. Maybe he and Logan had more in common than he first supposed.

Bridger spotted a familiar face over her shoulder. "Is that your aunt?" He pointed to the couple standing near the hostess's stand, waiting to be seated.

Maggie angled. Eyes wide, she turned to face him. "It *is* Aunt G." Her voice dropped to a whisper. "And who's the man with her?"

He shrugged, but she'd already whipped around again. "Aunt G!" She waved.

Menus in hand, the hostess was leading the distinguished-looking older gentleman toward a table on the far side of the restaurant.

Hearing her name, GeorgeAnne paused. Catching sight of them in the booth, she frowned. Maggie motioned her over.

Not appearing pleased to see them, GeorgeAnne said something to her escort but came over to speak to them. "Fancy meeting you four here."

Maggie pursed her lips. "What are you doing here?"

GeorgeAnne sniffed. "Eating same as you, what else?"

The older gentleman sidled up to Maggie's aunt and put a light hand on her sleeve. "Georgie, they've got our table ready."

And the seventyish doyenne of Truelove turned seven shades of red. But before introductions could be made, the hostess pulled him away with a question.

"Georgie?" Maggie fluttered her lashes. "Have you been holding out on us, Aunt G?"

"You just hush." The old woman wagged her finger. "Walter—"

"Walter, is it?" Maggie crowed.

GeorgeAnne pushed her glasses farther along the bridge of her nose. "If you must know, Miss Nosy—"

"Oh, that's rich." Maggie smirked. "Coming from the Queen of Nosy."

GeorgeAnne's mouth became prim. "AnnaBeth Stone introduced us a few months ago. Walter is a retired judge. We keep company on Friday nights. He takes me to dinner."

"Far enough out of town you're not likely to run into anyone you know." Mischief sparked in Maggie's eyes. "I'm scandalized, Aunt G. What would Miss IdaLee or Miss ErmaJean think?"

"None of their business is what I think." GeorgeAnne's mouth thinned. "If you're done having your fun at my expense, Mary Margaret, Walter is waiting for me."

"Have fun, Aunt G." She winked. "But not too much fun."

GeorgeAnne snorted. Head held high, she sailed away without another word.

Maggie laughed. "I never thought I'd live to see the day GeorgeAnne Allen was speechless."

He reached for the check. "Love, it does make the world go round."

She looked down and then up at him out of the corner of her eyes. "So I've heard." She gave him a small smile.

At the store, he and Maggie each took a twin by the hand. Once they were in the shoe department, she let the boys wander free-range. "We're going to buy shoes tonight, guys."

He followed Logan down the aisle. "Which ones do you like?"

She ran herd on Austin. "How about you, honey?"

Logan pointed to the display shelf. "Me wike deez."

Bridger handed him the black pair of shoes with the

neon-green stripe. The shoes were a type of sneaker sandal. Clutching a similar but bright blue pair to his chest, Austin clambered onto the padded stool.

She hurried after him. "You want to try them on to see if they fit?"

His blond curls bobbed. "Yeah."

"First, we have to take your other shoes off."

Austin pulled back the Velcro strap across his sandals. "Deez awe bwroken."

Bridger helped Logan remove his old shoes. "Your shoes aren't broken. You're just getting new ones for the summer."

Crouching, she helped Austin slip his foot into the sneaker. "You can wear your new shoes to the park."

Logan perked. "To my birfday?"

"Where else?" Squatting beside Maggie, Bridger tapped his finger on the little boy's nose. "'Cause you're the birthday boy."

He exchanged a secret smile with Maggie. The twins were going to love the birthday party she'd planned. After borrowing a few tools from Ethan's woodworking shop, Bridger couldn't wait to unveil his big birthday gift for the boys.

Of course, he had to finish making it first.

Austin dangled his feet, admiring the view. "Wear to splash-splash, too?"

Bridger raised his brow into a question mark, waiting for Maggie to interpret.

"There's a slip-n-slide water park in Charlotte. Anna-Beth took Hunter there when they visited her mother. The twins heard about how fun it is."

Logan nodded. "Splash-splash."

She pulled Austin to his feet. "Stand still and let me

see how much room your big toe has." She pressed her thumb to the top of his shoe. "Maybe I could take them to the water park later in the summer."

He checked Logan's toes. "Sounds like fun. On one condition, though."

She sat on her heels. "What's that?"

"I want to go, too."

She smiled. "You may live to regret that offer."

Rising, he offered his hand to help her to stand. "I won't."

"All right, guys." She gestured toward the end of the aisle. "Let's see how you walk in them."

The twins took off running.

He chuckled. "Running works, too."

"Not so far!" She nudged him. "Now you see why shoe shopping with toddler twins is a tag-team event."

"Got it." He moved to intercept the twins. "Come this way, guys."

Turning on their heels, they dashed back.

She took Logan's hand. "Do the shoes feel good?"

"Yeah."

He caught hold of Austin. "Not too tight?"

"No."

"Look at me." Kneeling, she got in front of their faces. "Any blisters?"

"No bwisters, Magwee." Austin smiled. "Me wike dem."

Bridger snagged their old sandals off the floor. "Should we buy them, then?"

Logan clapped his hands. "Buy. Buy. Buy."

"There you have it." She handed each twin an empty shoebox to carry. "Let's go pay for the shoes."

Austin stopped beside a pair of tiny work boots. "Me wike deez, too."

Bridger cocked his head. "I have a pair like that. Matching shoes, guys. How cool would that be?"

"I love the idea." She laughed. "But those aren't shoes for summer, Austin."

"Maybe we can come back at the end of summer and buy those, too." He smiled. "With Maggie's help."

Warmth filled her eyes.

Bridger wanted her to know that after his mother returned, he and the boys still wanted her company.

Handing over his credit card at the checkout counter, he went into sticker shock. "Seriously? How soon will they outgrow these?" He scratched his head.

Walking to the parking lot, she kept a firm grip on both twins while he tucked his card into his wallet.

She laughed. "Dad used to joke Mom worked part-time to keep me in shoes. And there was only one of me."

It was way past the boys' usual bedtime by the time Bridger finally turned onto the secondary road that led to town. The twins had fallen asleep in their car seats.

Working up his courage, he cleared his throat. "Why don't you scoot over here next to me? That way we won't disturb the boys."

A blatant exaggeration. Once the twins went to sleep, nothing woke them up. He didn't know if she'd reject his obvious ploy to get closer to her.

There was a long moment of silence. On his part, terror that he'd misstepped. Overstepped. Read her signals wrong.

But then, sliding over beside him, she buckled herself into the middle seatbelt. And he let himself take a full breath. He felt somehow he'd overcome yet another invisible hurdle of trust with her.

Faces lit by the glow of the dashboard, they talked quietly. Getting to know each other better. Learning each other's likes and dislikes about movies, books, food. Laughing softly.

Eventually the conversation wound down. But the silence was comfortable. When he placed his hand on the seat between them, she twined her fingers through his.

"C-can I ask you something, Bridger?"

He flicked a look in her direction. "Anything." He squeezed her hand.

"What do you know about Austin and Logan's birth mother?"

His head reared a fraction. Hadn't seen that question coming. "I know everything I need to know about her."

Bridger didn't like thinking about before the boys became Hollingsworths.

"Some girl got herself into trouble." He shifted on the seat. "Gave them up. Walked away. She has nothing to do with them now."

Maggie had gone still. "But one day—" she sounded hoarse "—don't you think they'll be curious? They might ask—"

"That woman should never show her face around here." He jutted his jaw. "We're their real family. Family is more than blood."

Slipping her hand free, she wrapped her arms around herself.

"Too much air? Are you cold?" He reached for the controls. "I'll turn the fan down a notch."

Somehow space on the seat had opened between them. Almost home, he asked her about her plans for

Saturday. Her voice low, she reminded him about Callie's baby shower.

"Oh, yeah. The boys are going fishing with your dad. Ethan, Jake and Jonas are dropping by to help me finish work on the birthday surprise."

At the house, she edged quietly out of the cab.

"I'll carry the twins to bed. You get on home." Shuffling his feet, he hated for the evening to end. "I never knew shoe shopping with toddlers could be so entertaining. But more than that, it was wonderful to talk with you." He stuck his hands in his pockets.

She nodded. Her face was a lovely oval, pale in the moonlight.

It was only later, while tucking the boys into bed, when a small niggle of worry began to gnaw at him. Things had been going so well with Maggie. But he'd sensed a shift there at the end.

He wasn't sure why, but he'd felt her withdraw from him. To the place where she held her feelings, thoughts and heart tightly shut away.

Bridger racked his memory for when the change had occurred. A subtle change, but real. He had an awareness when it came to her.

He'd never experienced that with any other woman. He'd never so wanted to please any woman more than Maggie. Most of all, though, he wanted her to be happy.

And that was when he put his finger on the emotion he sensed before she left. A deep core of unhappiness. Something more than the emotional scars he'd carried from his failed relationship with Chelsea. Something stemming from her past—the past she didn't want to talk about.

Whatever it was, it continued to hurt Maggie. Everybody struggled with something. And he resolved to be there for her.

Because of his growing feelings for her, seeing her in pain and walking away was not going to be an option for him.

Chapter Nine

On Saturday afternoon, Callie's baby shower was in full swing when Maggie arrived.

Lorena was hosting the occasion for her stepdaughter at her brick midcentury-modern home, which had a gorgeous panoramic view of the surrounding mountains.

Maggie had lain awake into the wee hours of the night pondering Bridger's harsh words about the twins' birth mother. Though he didn't know it, harsh words about her.

Prodded by guilt and a desire to be truthful, she'd felt enough confidence in his regard for her to tentatively broach the subject. His response had in no uncertain terms given her a clear picture of where he stood on the issue of the boys' biological mother.

Leaving her more confused than ever. And terrified she'd lose her sons again. She'd made a lifetime habit of trying to do the right thing. But this? The more time she spent with them, the more she got to know them and they her—losing them wasn't something she could bear to even contemplate.

Venturing inside Lorena's house, she clutched her

gift, wrapped in baby blue paper. In a seat of honor, Callie waved as she dug into a gift bag bedecked with jungle animals. In a nearby chair, Amber recorded the gifts in a notebook.

Excited about her new baby brother, Callie's four-year-old daughter hovered near her mother's elbow with the all-important job of transferring opened gifts to a display table. Under Miss IdaLee's direction, of course.

Training in the niceties of polite society started early for Southern girls. Watching little Maisie interact with the very prim but nurturing eightyish schoolmarm, Maggie hid her smile. It did indeed take a village. And the village of Truelove took its child-rearing responsibilities seriously.

One of the more endearing qualities of her hometown. Everyone might know your business. But in a small town, they were also there to lend a hand and help you celebrate life's most wonderful celebrations, too.

Glancing at the elegant party decor—AnnaBeth's contribution—Maggie reckoned a month ago she would've never imagined herself attending a baby shower. She no longer dreaded events such as these. Since the boys came into her life, so much had changed for her. Bridger's face rose in her mind. Not only because of the twins.

"We're putting gifts over there." Munching on a cheese straw, her aunt motioned toward the pile of unopened presents, stacked on a lace-covered table. "We've set the food out in the dining room."

Beside her on the sofa, her aunt's two compatriots in matchmaking mischief called out greetings.

A few minutes later, she returned to the gathering, her plate loaded with homemade party food and a cake prepared by Callie's friends. A labor of love. Maggie had dropped her contribution off earlier for GeorgeAnne to bring—toasted pecans gathered last fall from the tree in front of her house.

Maggie's gift sat on Callie's shrinking lap. "Come over and talk to me," the mother-to-be beckoned.

Edging past the matchmakers, she found a vacant spot on the nearby love seat. Callie slid a finger underneath the tape on the wrapping paper.

Amber sighed loudly. "Callie Rose McAbee, if you don't start tearing into these presents, I'm going call my girls to do it for you."

Everyone, including Callie, laughed.

Maggie took a sip of punch. "I didn't realize Lucy and Stella were here, too."

"Because you didn't hear them, you mean." Amber's eyes twinkled. "AnnaBeth has them occupied decorating their own cupcakes in the kitchen."

"Bless the child." GeorgeAnne pursed her lips. "And I'm not speaking of the twins."

ErmaJean gave her lifelong friend a cool look. "Those *wonderful* twin kindergartners are my beloved great-granddaughters."

"Speaking of twins?" Maggie hastened to intervene before a matchmaker tiff erupted. "Austin and Logan picked out the gift themselves for Truelove's newest little edition."

Callie removed the box lid. "Which makes the gift all the more special." She folded back the tissue. "Oh, look how sweet." She held up the onesie with the embroidered green tractor. "Jake will love this."

Maggie smiled. "Logan remembered riding the tractor at the ice-cream social."

"Look, Mommy!" Maisie lifted the matching green ball cap from the box. "Our baby will be so, so cute."

Maggie grinned, pleased they liked the gift. "Austin's contribution." Her lips twitched. "Baby McAbee will have to grow into the cap. Austin picked the cap to fit his own head."

Everyone chuckled.

Amber threw Maggie a teasing look. "Unlike me, Callie won't get to discover the joy of twins for herself."

Her heart skipped a beat. Unlike her, too.

Callie hugged her daughter. "I think the baby, Maisie, Jake and I are perfect just as we are."

Perfect. That was exactly what she felt when she was with Austin, Logan and Bridger. They were perfect together.

Callie winked at Maggie. "But I do want to hear every detail about those precious boys of yours."

She flushed. They weren't hers. Not really. Not the way Maisie belonged to Callie. Or Lucy and Stella belonged to Amber. And Hunter to AnnaBeth.

But they *were* hers. Even if no one but her ever knew. Yet like every mother on the planet, she couldn't resist bragging on about her little guys.

ErmaJean clapped her plump hands together. "I'm baking twin cakes for their birthday party next Saturday."

GeorgeAnne frowned.

After most of the guests took their leave, Maggie stayed behind to help Lorena put the house to rights. It took both Amber's and AnnaBeth's cars to load the gifts. They departed to follow Callie home. It didn't take long before Lorena's house was once again spick-and-span.

"Is it safe to come inside now?" Nash poked his graying blond head around the frame of the back door. "All the hens returned to their own coops?" He winked at Maggie. "You saved some cake for me, didn't you? Grandpas need food, too."

His much-beloved wife sighed. "Yes, my darling. Never fear. I have a large piece of cake with your name on it, waiting for you in the fridge."

Nash smiled. "Ice cream, too?"

Laughing, Maggie skipped out the door, leaving the second-time-around couple to enjoy their evening. She was surprised to find her aunt's truck still parked beside her car in the front yard. Window down, the old woman sat grim-faced behind the wheel.

She hurried forward. "Aunt G, are you—"

"Get in, Maggie." GeorgeAnne flicked the door lock. "You have some explaining to do."

It was only then she realized how uncharacteristically quiet her great-aunt had been toward the end of the shower.

Gut tightening, Maggie scrambled inside the truck. She pulled the door shut with a soft click.

A moment of strained silence ticked by. Her palms went damp.

GeorgeAnne twisted in her seat. "What have you done, Mary Margaret?" The old woman's face contorted. "What have you done?"

Maggie tucked a tendril that had come loose from her ponytail behind her ear. But her hand shook, and she quickly dropped it into her lap.

GeorgeAnne didn't know—she *couldn't* know.

She might have her suspicions, but suspicions did not

proof make. Yet Maggie had learned the hard way during various adolescent misdeeds, her aunt could be like a hound dog on the scent. The scent of truth.

"What's wrong, Aunt G?"

Her aunt's blue eyes glinted. "You know what's wrong."

She chewed her bottom lip. Whatever it was GeorgeAnne thought she'd done, it probably had nothing to do with the twins. But it would be wise to divert the old woman onto a safer path of inquiry.

Maggie opened her mouth, but GeorgeAnne beat her to the punch.

"Before you ask me how, I'll tell you how I know." The old lady's nostrils flared. "Birthday party. Twins. June 16."

She closed her eyes. ErmaJean had mentioned making Austin's and Logan's birthday cakes for next Saturday. No one knew the significance of those dates to Maggie.

No one, except her great-aunt.

Her worst fear realized. No—that wasn't true. Her worst fear would be realized if Bridger ever found out the truth.

Which he mustn't. Not ever. Too much was at stake. Not the least of which was any hope of a relationship with Bridger and, by extension, her sons.

She dug her nails into her palms. "You won't tell anyone, will you, Aunt G?"

GeorgeAnne glared. "Bridger deserves to hear the truth from you. If you truly love him, you can't keep something so important from him."

"L-love him?" She fell onto the seat. "I never said I loved him."

"There's none so blind as those who refuse to see."

GeorgeAnne's mouth thinned. "You two are beginning to wear on my last nerve."

Loved him? Was that what she felt for Bridger? Love?

Maggie shook her head. She admired him. She valued his friendship. He made her feel safe. He made her feel as if the past had never happened.

But it had. There was no undoing what happened then. Or now.

GeorgeAnne waved her hand. "I see the way you look at him. How he looks at you. You need to tell him the truth before he finds out on his own. He'll be angry, but if you explain—"

"He won't understand."

GeorgeAnne shook her head. "If you explain the circumstances—"

"You mean the truth about how their biological father attacked me?" Bile rose in her throat.

"Bridger is their father now. Just as God is their heavenly Father." Her aunt clasped her hands under her chin. "God loves those boys far more than even you love them. You can trust Him to take care of them and their future. But He will never honor lies."

"Telling Bridger also means explaining what happened to me in Atlanta." Her stomach cramped. "And if you're right about the way he looks at me, he'll never look at me that way again."

"Oh, Maggie." Lips quivering, GeorgeAnne looked away for a second before regaining her composure. "How can you think so little of him? Of yourself?"

"I never meant for any of this to happen, Aunt G." Her voice choked. "I only discovered the truth when I learned of Bridger's connection to their adoptive parents." Tears streaming down her face, she lifted her gaze. "Wilda's due home in a few weeks. And then maybe no one need ever know."

"Except the truth has an unfortunate habit of coming out at the worst possible moment. And Wilda has nothing to do with the feelings growing between you and Bridger. A relationship cannot survive when it's built upon lies."

"I'm not ready to tell him yet. Let me have these last weeks with my sons."

"This isn't going to end well." GeorgeAnne gathered Maggie's hands in her work-worn palms. "Not for Bridger. Nor those sweet little boys. Most especially not for you."

"Please, Aunt G," Maggie pleaded.

GeorgeAnne's wrinkled features sagged. "After their birthday party next weekend, you'll tell him? Promise me, Mary Margaret."

"I promise," she whispered.

But it was a promise she wasn't sure she could keep.

The following Saturday, Bridger put the finishing touches on his surprise for the boys. And none too soon. The party started in a few hours.

With a whir of the cordless screwdriver, he tightened the last bolt on the sloping wooden pallet.

"That's a wrap." Ethan set the last paver stone in place on the ground. "Looks great if I do say so myself." He grinned.

Jonas gathered his tools. "Nothing wrong with his self-esteem."

Bridger laughed.

Jonas was closest in age to him, and he'd enjoyed getting to know the quiet, soft-spoken cowboy. But Ethan was correct about the tiny-tyke obstacle course they'd installed for the birthday party Maggie had planned for the twins.

Bridger had worked on it in bits and pieces during his spare time, but he could've never gotten everything done for the party without their help.

Jake had been unable to join them today. Overnight, he'd rushed Callie to the hospital. And this morning he was the proud father of a healthy baby boy. Callie and little Micah McAbee were doing well and resting comfortably.

Ethan's wife wandered outside. "Self-esteem?" Amber sniffed. "Jonas is too kind. Don't know that's the word I'd have chosen."

Wrapping his arm around her waist, Ethan tugged her close. "You know you love me."

"Sure do." She patted his cheek. "But probably not as much as you love yourself."

AnnaBeth and Maggie came out to the backyard at the same moment Ethan lunged for his wife. Squealing in mock terror, Amber ran away.

Catching Bridger's eye, Maggie shook her head at their antics. But a smile tugged the corners of her mouth. He liked her friends.

Amber didn't go far before Ethan grabbed her around the waist again. "Caught you."

She turned in his arms. "'Cause I let you."

Ethan kissed her forehead. "Just so long as you keep letting me catch you."

Something stirred in Bridger's heart. Despite the kidding around, there was no mistaking the love shining from Amber's and Ethan's faces. Their journey to happiness had been a road fraught with misunderstandings, but all had come right in the end.

Would he ever experience anything close to the kind of marriage they enjoyed? His eyes flicked toward Maggie.

Coming off the porch, she hugged Amber. "Thanks for everything."

"That's what friends are for." Her arm tucked into the crook of Ethan's arm, Amber leaned her head against his shoulder as they made their exit.

Maggie hugged AnnaBeth. "What would I have done without you?"

Jonas kissed the top of his wife's red hair. "I feel like that every day." Calling goodbye, they headed out, too.

"I didn't know things could be like that between a man and a woman." With a start, he realized he'd said out loud what he'd been thinking.

"How is it with everything you've seen as a cop, you still believe in happily-ever-after?"

At the wistful note in her voice, he faced her. "Because of everything I've seen in my line of work, I find I *must* believe in happily-ever-after."

Slowly, afraid to spook her, he lifted his hand. He held it in front of her face so he wouldn't startle her.

When she didn't move away, he ran his thumb over the apple of her cheek. "Do you believe happily-ever-after is possible, Maggie?"

"I didn't use to." Her lashes swept upward. "But now…" She moistened her lips. "I hope so." She lifted her mouth to his. "Oh, how I hope so."

When she placed her hand on his chest, he went still. Surely she could feel the thumping vibration of his heart through his shirt. Did this mean he'd finally won her trust?

Did this mean she might be starting to feel something for him?

He took a deep breath. "Maggie?"

With the other women he'd dated, he hadn't felt the need to declare his intentions. It had just happened between them. The occasion—the women—hadn't warranted such carefulness.

But this was Maggie. She was special. So strong. So precious. So fragile. He wouldn't do anything to jeopardize what he felt building between them.

He was filled with hope for a future he'd only just begun to believe possible for him. A future he'd only just acknowledged he wanted. With her. With the boys. Someday... And this, the first step.

"Yes, Bridger?"

She looked at him, a question in those luminous brown eyes of hers. Eyes he believed he might drown in if he ever lowered his protective guards. If he ever found the courage to go all in with another relationship.

"Can I kiss you?"

He died a thousand deaths in the three seconds before she replied. Doubted what his instincts told him to be true. Doubted himself. Despite her playfulness with him and the twins, sometimes she could be so remote.

She was a puzzle he might spend a lifetime unraveling.

She placed her hands atop his shoulders. "Kiss me, Bridger."

His heart hammered. She wanted him to kiss her.

Not making any sudden moves, he raised his hands and placed them on either side of her face. The clean, natural smell of her was as unassuming as she was. Yet intoxicating to his senses.

He pulled her closer. Only a hairbreadth separated them. She closed her eyes.

Lowering his head, he brushed his lips across hers. Holding her loosely, he pulled back a fraction, giving her the option to stop him at any time. He wanted her to feel in control. More than anything in the world, he wanted her to trust him.

Her eyelashes fluttered. "Is that all you have to say for yourself, Chief Hollingsworth?" She wound her hands around his neck.

Bridger gave her a lopsided smile. "Matter of fact, it's not. Not by a long shot."

Kissing her again, his lips were gentle. Then she surprised him by kissing him back. It was a sweetness he could have never imagined. She fit into his arms as if she'd been made for him. And he for her.

Only with regret did he finally come up for air. He stared at her upturned face. What he felt had been so... so much more than he'd ever imagined himself feeling, he had to swallow past the unaccustomed emotion clogging his throat.

"How was that?" he rasped.

Opening her eyes, a pleased smile flickered across her features. "Nearly as perfect as I imagined." Heat bloomed in her cheeks.

"You've been imagining, have you?" he teased.

She started to drop her gaze, but cupping her face, he resisted her attempt to shut him out.

"Nearly perfection, you said?" He grinned. "Gives me something to aim for next time."

It took every ounce of self-discipline not to give in to the urge to kiss her again right then and there.

But they were operating on borrowed time. He was surprised Tom hadn't returned with the twins already. Or that the birthday guests and their moms hadn't interrupted them.

"Next time?" she whispered.

He grazed his mouth against the skin on the back of her hand. "Would a next time be okay with you?"

When she smiled, he believed his heart would gallop out of his chest.

"Yes," she said. "It most definitely would."

Chapter Ten

The next few hours passed in a whirlwind of activity.

After their fishing expedition, Maggie's dad brought the boys back to the house for the party.

Bridger stood behind Austin on a stool at the kitchen sink. Her son held his hands under the running water of the faucet.

For all practical purposes, however, Austin kept pumping the liquid soap and squishing it between his palms. Sudsy bubbles floated upward. But she applauded Bridger for his valiant, if vain, attempt to bring a semblance of hygiene to the wiggly blond twin.

Bridger shook his head and glanced over his shoulder at her dad. "I can't imagine how you got these two to actually sit still long enough to fish." His eyes flitted to her and lingered.

So handsome in his black basketball shorts, sneakers and a dark gray T-shirt. Her heart did a funny, achy staccato. Smiling, she put the last of the items into the goody bags each child would take home after the party.

"They don't sit still. Dad takes their shoes and socks off. They all—including big kid Dad—wade into the creek up to their ankles. They jump and yell and giggle when the minnows nip their toes. And then Dad lets them take turns holding his fishing pole."

Her father grinned. "Young fishermen in the making."

"And here I thought fishing was a quiet, contemplative hobby." Bridger scratched his head. "Not sure how much actual fishing or contemplating gets done, though."

Tom laughed. "There's nothing wrong with their lungs, that's for sure."

Soon after, the rest of the twins' Tumbling Tots friends arrived with their moms or dads. To Maggie's surprise, GeorgeAnne's truck also pulled into the long gravel drive. She was even more surprised when Erma-Jean and IdaLee hopped out, as well.

GeorgeAnne marched toward the porch. "Figured you could use the help."

She wasn't wrong.

With everyone gathered in the backyard, Maggie handed each child a stretchy blue headband, coordinating with the red, white and blue decorations, goody bags and balloons.

Bridger cut his eyes at her. "Why do I get the feeling you spent a lot more than the money I gave you for the party?"

Maggie patted his arm. "I wanted them to have the best birthday party ever." It amazed her how natural and right it felt to touch him so casually. "How much I spent of my own money is none of your business."

She never dreamed she'd ever get to throw her sons a birthday party. And once she told Bridger the truth, she might never get to do it again. So she'd gone all out.

She refused to think about what might happen after she told him. She was determined to fully enjoy today.

True to her storm-the-barricade nature, GeorgeAnne took charge. She positioned the small ninja warrior athletes at the starting point.

"Let ErmaJean blow the horn." GeorgeAnne threw a grin toward her old friend. "She's good at noise."

ErmaJean took GeorgeAnne's teasing in stride, same as she always did. By ignoring her.

Sporting hot-pink sneakers and her usual teacher skirt, Miss IdaLee walked down the lineup. "Be safe," she cautioned the children.

"Get ready." Gripping the handheld air horn, ErmaJean made sure she had everyone's attention. "Let the games begin!" She squeezed the horn, and the first child took off.

One by one each child was put through the paces of the obstacle course. On the sidelines, parents cheered the little contestants through each challenge. Cell phones ready, parents recorded their little ones' athletic triumphs from beginning to end. There was lots of encouragement.

The tiny ninja warriors hopped their way across the stepping-stones. They meandered across the sloping wooden pallets. Arms extended, they picked their way to the end of the ground-level balance beam.

"Such athleticism," Miss ErmaJean crowed.

After the beam, they crawled on their bellies underneath the two-foot staked PVC piping. And worked their way across a set of monkey bars, easily reached on tiptoe.

"Look at that upper-body strength," ErmaJean yelled. "Give it everything you got, kiddo."

Maggie and Bridger exchanged amused glances.

GeorgeAnne rolled her eyes. "She watches too much television."

For the grand finale, each child climbed the slightly sloped warp wall.

Holding a stopwatch, GeorgeAnne waited for them at the top. Grinning hugely, the pint-size ninjas each hit the red buzzer.

Since it was their party, Maggie had Austin and Logan run the course last. Of the twins, Logan went first. She smiled when Bridger whipped out his phone, too. Like the proud papa he was.

Her heart felt so full. Why had she ever doubted? He was a great dad to the boys.

When the horn blared, Logan took off.

"Go, go, go!" she screamed.

"You can do it," her father urged.

Miss IdaLee jumped up and down like a teenager. "He's almost to the warp wall."

"Faster! Faster!" Bridger called.

Logan took the wall at a run. Reaching the top, he slammed his hand on the buzzer. And stern, wound-tight GeorgeAnne nearly lost her mind. "Yes! Yes! Yes!" she screamed, waving the stopwatch.

All at once recollecting she was making a spectacle of herself, her great-aunt came down on her heels. "As I was saying…" She smoothed her iron-gray hair in place. "Well done, young Hollingsworth."

Logan's brown eyes flitted across the crowd till he found Maggie. His face gleamed with pride. "Look me, Magwee! Look me!" He stuck his thumb to his chest.

Her heart swelled with love.

With equal fervor, Austin ran the course last.

At the finish line, Bridger put him on his shoulder.

She'd created a playlist for this moment, including "We Are the Champions." Bridger and Austin led the rest of the little athletes around the perimeter in a victory lap.

She hung a ribbon medal around each child's neck.

Clapping her hands, ErmaJean called the children to find a seat at the table on the screened porch. "Cake time."

GeorgeAnne tapped her finger on the face dial of the stopwatch. "Our boys had the best times by far."

Our boys? Maggie's lips curved in a smile.

Her aunt jutted her bony chin. "Good mountain stock."

Parents and children headed toward the porch.

"Every kid gets a participation award?" Bridger's mouth quirked. "How very millennial of you, Maggie Arledge."

Before she could think of a snarky comeback, Miss IdaLee breezed by. "Let them be little."

Maggie pursed her lips. "Yeah. That. Chief Hollingsworth."

ErmaJean and IdaLee brought out the cakes and placed one in front of each boy.

Maggie positioned herself behind Austin, and Bridger stood behind Logan.

"Okay, guys." She lit the two candles on each cake. "One…two—"

"I can do one, two, free, Magwee." Logan held up his hand.

"Yes, you can." Bridger laughed. "Now blow out those candles, boys."

They tried… They really did try.

Lips quirking, Bridger shrugged. "Next year."

"Be my guest, Chief." She gestured at the flickering candles. "I think you're the one to finish the job."

He cocked his head. "'Cause I've got so much hot air to spare?"

Maggie laughed at him. "Your words, not mine."

He obliged. Everyone clapped.

ErmaJean came out of the kitchen carrying a large rectangular pan. "Sheet cake for the rest of us."

Maggie took funny photos of Austin's and Logan's faces smeared with chocolate frosting. She'd treasure the memories of this day forever.

The boys received lots of toys from the other boys and girls. And then they opened their gifts from Mr. Tom.

"Dad!" Her eyes widened when she saw what he'd gotten them. "Go overboard much?"

Her father looked sheepish, but Bridger grinned at the toddler-size fishing reels.

"I'd like to borrow the boys from time to time…" Her dad smiled. "Can't think of a better way to spend my retirement."

"Be my guest." Winking at her, Bridger folded his arms across his chest. "I'm sure I can find something to keep me occupied while they're gone."

Suddenly, it felt to Maggie that every eyeball zeroed in on her. Red crept up her neck. Bridger Hollingsworth was outrageous.

And wonderful. And heart-stoppingly attractive. And a host of other qualities she had only just begun to discover.

Eager to draw the spotlight off herself, though, she shoved more gifts at the twins. "Let's find out what's in here."

When it was time for their party guests to leave, Austin and Logan gave each of their little friends a hug.

"So, so sweet," one of the moms murmured.

The matchmakers and her father pitched in to clean up the kitchen and backyard. They'd no sooner departed than Bridger's phone buzzed on the counter.

"It's my mother." He read the message on the screen. "She wants to FaceTime and wish the twins a happy birthday."

Wiping her hands on the drying cloth, Maggie called the boys, playing with some of their birthday gifts on the braided rug in the living room.

At the sight of Nana on the cell phone screen, the twins were at first bewildered. But then delighted for a chance to talk with her, they tripped over each other's words to tell her about their exciting day.

Off-screen, Maggie gestured to remind them to thank their grandmother for the gifts Wilda had sent to them in the mail.

"I'll send you the videos I took, Mom," Bridger said, when he could finally get a word in edgewise.

"No rush." Wilda's shoulders rose and fell. "Tom already shared his with me."

Maggie widened her eyes at Bridger. Since when had Bridger's mother and her father gotten so chummy?

"It looks like it was an absolutely wonderful party, Maggie."

She jerked her attention to the phone Bridger had propped on the farm table.

Wilda smiled at her. "So many special touches. Thank you so much for making their second birthday so memorable."

"I love them so much, Miss Wilda." Her eyes welled unexpectedly. "I would do anything in the world for them."

And it was true. Although, no one but GeorgeAnne knew to what lengths she'd already gone. Her promise to tell Bridger everything lay like a boulder on her chest, heavy on her heart.

Was her aunt right? Would Bridger understand?

Bridger asked about his sister's health. Maggie used the opportunity to say goodbye. She moved to the drain board to put away the last of the dishes. And to gain control of her roller-coaster emotions.

Ending the call, Bridger and the twins drifted outside. Finishing up, Maggie wandered out to the screened porch. She collapsed into the swing. A bemused smile on his face, Bridger stood staring out at the backyard. The boys raced around on their new ninja course.

After a second, he eased down beside her. "I guess after all that sugar, they need to work off some energy."

Her heart quivered. It had been the best, most perfect day of her life. Was she being greedy?

God forgive her if she was, but she wanted more days like this. So many more. With Bridger. And her sons. As a family.

Her eyes darted to the man beside her. But would he give her that chance after she told him the truth? Did she deserve a second chance?

Sensing her scrutiny, he turned his head. He ran a hand over his beard stubble. "Something wrong with my face?"

There was absolutely nothing wrong with his face, or anything else about Bridger.

A buzzing began in her brain. This was it. This was the moment. She'd promised GeorgeAnne. Why did everything always have to be so hard?

She opened her mouth to tell him the biggest secret of her life, but nothing came out.

He gave her a smile. "What?"

And she chickened out.

"I—I wanted to stop by the hospital and see Callie's baby." She jumped to her feet, setting the swing in motion. "I should probably go."

He brought the rocking swing to rest and rose.

Only a hairbreadth separated them. So, so close. Recalling the last time they'd stood this close—was it only yesterday?—her cheeks flamed.

Perhaps he remembered, too. Placing his thumb and forefinger on her chin, he angled her face toward him. "I think this qualifies as next time. Don't you?"

Rising on her tiptoes, she smiled. "I do." And without waiting for him to make the first move, she kissed him.

His lips firm against hers, he tasted of spearmint gum. It was everything a kiss ought to be. He was a good man with honorable intentions. Also a man who respected her and loved her sons with all his heart.

Pulling back, he rested his forehead against hers. "Better this time?"

She smiled. "Perfect."

"I guess we'll have to find another way to spend our time since I've mastered kissing you." He inched back. "How do you feel about fishing?"

She play-smacked his biceps. "You are ridiculous."

Grinning, he rubbed his arm.

Apparently she had more girlie-girl in her than she ever suspected. Or maybe it was Bridger who brought that out in her.

She placed her finger on her chin. "On second thought…"

He arched his eyebrow.

"Perhaps I was too quick to proclaim perfection. Close to excellent, but not yet splendid."

He grinned. "I can work with that."

"Till next time, then?"

"Till then."

After Maggie left, the twins' sugar highs crashed.

Bridger was left with a couple of whiny, overly tired birthday boys. They also needed a bath. Even on a good day, that was a challenging endeavor.

Today, it was all he could do to wrestle his twin alligators into the tub. Then he had an idea. A brilliant idea, courtesy of Maggie.

If she wasn't above stooping to bribery, why shouldn't he? Desperate times called for desperate measures.

"Guys…" Palms upturned and hands wide, he approached the boys the same way he'd coax a jumper on a ledge. "How about if you help me with your bath, I'll read you the book you and Maggie love so much?"

Austin looked at Logan. Logan looked at Austin. Considered his offer. Weighed the pros and cons. Bridger held his breath and prayed.

"Okay." Logan opened his small chubby hands. "We do it."

He had the sense he'd just been awarded a gracious concession. Whatever worked, though. Right?

It wasn't as bad as he feared. Or else, the boys took pity on him. Eventually, they were clean and in their pajamas, smelling of soap. Like warm bundles on either side of him, they reclined against the pillows on his big bed to read the story.

He'd seen Maggie read this book to them over and over. He spotted an inscription written on the inside cover. The only word he caught of the inscription was *Mother*. Impatient, Austin flipped past to the first page.

It was a sweet book about a mother's forever love. By the time he turned the last page, the boys were drowsy, their eyelids heavy.

Bridger closed the book. "'The end.'" He planted a quick kiss on first the dark head and then the blond one. "Time for bed, guys."

One at a time, he carried them to their beds. Tucking the covers around them, he snuggled them against his chest once more. Then standing between the beds, he gazed at the sleeping twins.

His boys. His sons. And his heart brimmed, full of gratitude, for the precious gifts God had entrusted to him. Forget the adrenaline of undercover work. Nothing topped the thrill of being their dad.

Bridger sighed. That was what he was. Austin and Logan's dad.

Flicking off the light switch, he went looking for a snack. After the noisy, wonderful day, the house was quiet. For the first time, he allowed himself to acknowledge his loneliness.

Sticking to the refrigerator door, he found a handwritten, lime-green note Maggie had somehow found the time to compose.

Till next time,
M

His stomach did a flutter flop. Maggie and her endearing notes. Being with her sparked joy somewhere deep inside him.

Retreating to his recliner, he found himself reflecting on the day. The last few weeks. The last year.

God had been good to him. Preserving his life

through some tough situations. Bringing him back to his faith, despite tragedy. Bringing him here to this job. This town.

To Maggie.

He was thankful for the friends and family God had placed in his life. None more so than Maggie. He'd never met another woman like her.

Strong, tough, beautiful Maggie. Not a dishonest bone in her body, she loved his boys as if they were her own. She was the most genuine person he'd ever met.

When he was with her, his loneliness retreated. Swallowed up by her zest for living. Her energy. She was sunshine after the rain.

He felt ready, brave enough, to take the next step. In some ways, it felt very much like stepping off the ledge of a building.

Stepping off in faith, yet not into nothingness. But into something more wonderful than he ever believed possible. And he found the courage to believe his heart might be safe in the hands of a woman.

If that woman was Maggie.

Chapter Eleven

Maggie meant to tell Bridger the truth, but somehow over the next few days, time got away from her. Due to a domestic conflict that required his attention as police chief, he was in and out that week. Too often, they were like ships passing in the night.

If they did manage to be in the same place at the same time, the boys were always with them. This definitely wasn't the type of conversation she wanted to start with that distraction, no matter how endearing the twins were.

And so it went. Or at least, that was the excuse she made to herself each night as she fell into bed. Full of self-recrimination, she knew she was dragging her feet. Allowing another day and another opportunity to slip through her fingers.

But whenever she felt the urge to tell him everything, her gut-level reluctance kicked in. And she rationalized that this moment with Bridger and the boys was too special to spoil. Or too fun. Too anything.

Later. She promised herself she'd do it later that day. Or that night. On and on it went. Before she realized it, an entire week had flown by. And it was Saturday again.

Headed over to see her guys—all her guys—on that late-June morning, she told herself in no uncertain terms she had to get serious about talking to Bridger.

Bridger's sister and her new baby were doing well. He'd decided to wait a few weeks before visiting with the twins. With Shannon's husband due back from his deployment soon, Wilda planned to return to Truelove early next week. It would be far better if Maggie's secret was out in the open before his mother returned.

When she arrived at the Hollingsworth home, Bridger and the boys were in the driveway. Setting down a brown plastic bucket, he gave her that slow, slightly crooked grin of his.

As she got out of the car, her stomach fluttered. Dressed in shorts and T-shirts, Austin and Logan stood next to the cruiser. A green water hose lay uncurled at their bare feet.

Her heart turned over. She loved, loved, loved little kid feet. So sweet. So innocent. So cute.

"Magwee! Magwee!" Jumping, hopping, skipping along the pavement, the boys enfolded her legs in an exuberant hug.

She kissed the tops of their heads.

"Good timing." Bridger raised a large yellow sponge. "The twins and I were about to give the cruiser a bath."

"Hmm…" She tapped her finger on her chin. "I think I just remembered somewhere else I'm supposed to be right now."

Bridger folded his arms across his chest. "Not so fast, Arledge. There's a sponge here with your name on it." His muscles bunched and flexed through the forest green T-shirt. *Be still, my heart.*

"The twins were looking forward to some Maggie time." He winked. "Me, too."

She cut her eyes at him. "When you put it that way—"

He smirked.

"I can take them on a run while you finish the car. And then maybe pencil you in on my calendar for next week."

At his expression, she couldn't help but laugh. "I'm teasing." A child standing on each of her feet, she slogged forward. "I'd love to help you wash your car. Love. Love. Love."

He rolled his eyes. "No need to lay it on so thick."

"Let's do it, guys." She disentangled herself from the twins. "Let the car washing commence."

Bridger went to find more sponges and drying cloths. Squirting dishwashing detergent in the bucket, she started filling the bucket with water from the hose. Until Austin fell into it and turned the bucket over.

Car washing—take two.

This time she let Austin squirt the liquid into the bucket. And then helped Logan squeeze the handle of the hose to fill the bucket. Both boys practically danced with glee at the sight of the rising soap bubbles.

Until Logan forgot what he was supposed to be doing, and released his hold on the handle. Writhing like a cobra, the hose sprayed both boys in the face.

Wiping the moisture from his eyes, Austin became indignant. Logan took exception to his indignation. A twin tussle ensued.

Bridger chose that moment to reappear. A good thing, since intervening in a twin squabble required tag-team action.

Car washing—take three.

She gave them their own sponge and banished each boy to opposite sides of the vehicle. Squatting beside the tires, they settled down and got to "work." She and Bridger stationed themselves on both sides of the cruiser to ensure no further hostilities arose.

She concentrated on cleaning the doors. "Only two years old, and already they have such fragile male egos." She arched her eyebrow. "My, my, my."

Taller by half a foot, Bridger wiped his foamy sponge across the roof of the cruiser. "I'll have my hands full. Could probably use a woman's influence." Moving to the hood, he cocked his head. "Know anyone brave enough to help out an outnumbered single dad?"

"I might know someone." She swiped the sponge over the half of the windshield she could reach. "Provided the price is right."

He laughed, low in his throat. "Name your price."

"Lots of hugs and kisses from my two favorite twins—"

"Just from the twins?"

She flushed. And a warm feeling curled in her belly.

Grinning, he sponged the other half of the windshield.

"Maybe a picnic or two with a certain police chief." She cast her gaze skyward, pretending to think. "And perhaps ice cream thrown in for good measure."

"Cwream?" Austin's voice piped from somewhere below. "Cwream?"

Moseying around the car, Logan tugged Bridger's cargo shorts. "We wuv cwream, Daddy."

Bridger shook his head. "Now you've done it."

Her lips twitched. "We need to finish helping Daddy—"

Bridger grinned.

"—wash his car." She loved how he loved them calling him Daddy. "After rest time, we can go get some ice cream, okay?"

"'Kay." Austin applied himself with renewed fervor to scouring the tire rim.

Logan returned to his set of tires. "We help."

"Just so I know what I'm agreeing to…" Bridger sudsed the side mirror. "A picnic?"

She wiped the window. "Or two."

He laid down his sponge. "A private interview with the police chief, you said?"

She fought the urge to grin. "If that's how you choose to spend that nickel."

He stuck his tongue in his cheek. "And a little *i-c-e c-r-e-a-m*."

"Or a lot." She smiled. "But spelling won't work for long. These little guys are smart."

He picked up the hose. "Good thing I've got you to advise me."

She gave him a sideways glance. "Good thing."

"Great job, Logan. Stand back." Bridger sprayed the tire. "Thanks so much for your help."

Dirty, soapy water ran off the rim, flowing in rivulets down the driveway. Logan clapped.

Coming around the car, Bridger hosed off Austin's tires. But in true Austin fashion, he got up close and personal. Slapping his feet on the pavement, he squished the runoff between his toes.

She sighed. "What is it with boys and water?"

"Is it just boys?" Bridger stopped spraying. "Maybe pretty girls like water, too?"

She didn't like the look of mischief in his eyes. "Bridger…"

"What?"

Narrowing her eyes, she raised her dripping sponge. "Don't."

"Don't what?" He feigned a look of innocence. "You're not scared of a little water, are you, sweetheart?"

The *sweetheart* caught her by surprise, but she wasn't fooled by his attempt to distract her.

She backed up a step. "Don't you dare, Hollingsworth."

Squeezing the handle, he sent a warning spritz across the car. Carefully aimed, it fell just shy of her sneakers.

Maggie jumped. "I mean it, Bridger…" She threw the sponge at him.

Ducking, he ran toward her, letting loose a stream of water.

Squealing, she dashed around the car with him hot on her heels. Water spattered the back of her shirt. He was gaining.

Like a couple of kids, she and Bridger raced around the cruiser. The two-year-olds had gone stock-still. Eyes big at the silliness of the so-called grown-ups.

"Austin! Logan!" She threw up her hands. "Help me!"

Giggling at this fun game, the boys began running in circles around the cruiser, but in the opposite direction. Facing an imminent collision with the twins, she stopped. Allowing Bridger to corner her against the bumper.

"Austin!" she pleaded. "Logan!"

The boys stationed themselves on either side of Bridger.

"What do you think, guys?" He looked at them. "Do we let Maggie go, or does Maggie need a bath?"

Chortling, Austin bounced on his tiptoes. But frowning, Logan held out his little hand.

After a second's hesitation, Bridger placed the handle in his palm. Logan smiled.

She sagged in relief. "Thank you, Lo—"

Logan squeezed the handle.

Water squirted into her face. Drenching her hair and shirt. She gasped.

"Me do," Austin cried. "Me."

Bridger about split a gut laughing. Until twin differences were forgiven and forgotten, Logan handed the hose to his twin. Who thoroughly doused their daddy, head to toe.

Sputtering, Bridger swiped the water from his face.

The next few minutes of capture-the-hose resulted in general mayhem. The boys weighing him down in a leg lock, she was giving Truelove's police chief a long-overdue rinse when a car door slammed.

"Land of lakes, what's going on here?"

Bridger's jaw dropped. "Mom?"

Wilda planted her hands on her hips. "I go away for two months, and y'all go crazy." Her eyes sparkled with merriment.

Maggie dropped the hose.

Hitting the concrete, the hose kinked. A final spurt of water jetted out. With a small cry and remarkable agility, Wilda hopped backward.

"I am so sorry." Hands outstretched, Maggie stepped toward her. "I never meant—"

But Wilda was laughing. At the spigot, Bridger cranked the water off. Two very damp twins rushed toward their grandmother, engulfing her with hugs and kisses.

Crinkling her nose, she patted the boys' heads. "No offense, but y'all smell like a bunch of wet dogs."

"We weren't expecting you till next week, Mom."

She winked at Maggie. "I can get in the car and return to Fayetteville, if you'd rather."

"No, of course not, Mom." Sheepish, he moved closer. "We're thrilled to have you with us again." He went to give his mother a hug.

Making a face, she cautiously offered her cheek. "You need a bath, too."

Austin perked.

Wilda held up her finger. "And I mean more than the water hose."

Maggie caught sight of her reflection in the window of the SUV. Scraping back her hair, she grimaced. "A great idea. But first, how's Shannon?"

"Wonderful. That's why I was able to return to Truelove earlier than planned." Wilda smiled. "Mission accomplished, her husband's squad returned stateside yesterday. I decided to give the proud papa space to get reacquainted with his family again."

"I'm happy Paul's home and safe." Bridger nodded. "I'll give them a call tomorrow."

"Good idea." Wilda became brisk. "Here's another good idea. Bridger and I can wrangle the twins into a bath. Maggie, why don't you head home and get changed? Tom and I thought we'd take the boys to town for some *i-c-e c-r-e-a-m*."

Somehow Wilda had gotten the spelling memo. No surprise Nana was way ahead of them.

His mother gave her a smile. "Then you and Bridger can have some time together."

But Maggie was still stuck on her mention of Tom. As in Maggie's dad? Apparently, her father and Wilda had kept in touch more than anyone realized. Perhaps absence did make the heart grow fonder.

Following on the heels of the parent epiphany came another equally startling revelation. Her father and Wilda saw Maggie and Bridger as a couple, deserving of alone time.

Her eyes darted to him. Did he think of them as a couple, too?

"I think that's an inspired idea, Mom." He flashed Maggie a grin. "I'm not going to turn down a chance to take my favorite twin sitter on a real date."

So perhaps he did see them as a couple.

"Our first official date." He broadened his chest. "But not our last."

A date with Bridger. *Wow. Just wow.* Butterflies did loop-do-loops in her belly.

They made quick plans for him to pick her up in a few hours. Back home, she found her father splashing on aftershave, looking pleased with himself in the bathroom mirror.

Crossing her arms, she leaned against the doorframe. "So, Dad, heading out to have ice cream with Wilda?"

He glanced at her in the mirror. "I like ice cream."

She gave up the attempt to look stern and hugged his arm. "I'm guessing you like Wilda, too."

"You don't mind?"

She smiled. "Not at all. The Hollingsworths are good people."

"Good taste, too." Her father tapped the end of her

nose. "Judging from the amount of time they spend with us Arledges." Cell beeping, he picked the phone off the sink and glanced at the screen. "Uh-oh."

"What?"

"The twins' car seats are in your car."

"Oh…right."

Her dad gave her a peck on the cheek. "No worries. I'll unhook the seats, take them with me and transfer them to Wilda's car. Won't affect you and Bridger at all."

"Thanks, Dad."

Forty minutes later, she was still debating—and agonizing—over what to wear. Why didn't she have anything special enough to wear on a date—a first date—with Bridger? She wanted to look good for him tonight.

For the first time in her life, she wished she was one of those girlie-girls who liked shopping for clothes. An AnnaBeth thing, not a Maggie thing.

Although, next time she'd be better prepared. A hum of anticipation sent goose bumps across her skin. She'd schedule a shopping trip to Asheville at AnnaBeth's earliest convenience.

Suddenly, it hit her that their time together—just the four of them—had ended with Wilda's return. But she was full of hope for her relationship with Bridger. And feeling more confident of a continuing place in her sons' lives, Wilda's return didn't spark the fear or panic it might once have kindled.

However, she'd still not broached the all-important secret of her real relationship to the boys with Bridger. She blew out a breath, fogging the glass partition. This was where her procrastination had landed her.

Nobody's fault but her own. She'd tell him tonight when they were alone. Her stomach clenched.

Or not.

She didn't want to spoil their first date. There was plenty of time. Tomorrow, maybe?

After church tomorrow, she'd invite Bridger to go hiking with her to a favorite local waterfall. Just the two of them. Then she'd tell him. Full disclosure.

No more secrets.

The next hour was a whirlwind of baths and wrestling two-year-olds into clean clothes. In small batches of interrupted conversation, Bridger and his mom caught up with each other.

Noses pressed to the front window, the twins watched for Tom's truck. He helped his mother pack their backpack in case the boys had an accident while out of the house.

"I really like Maggie." His mother gave him a pensive smile. "She's everything I prayed for you, honey. Since you were the twins' age."

He swallowed. "I—I like her, too."

"She's so good with the boys." His mom zipped the backpack. "She'll make some man a good wife."

Bridger propped against the counter. "You don't say?"

His mother slung the strap over her shoulder. "Can't understand why some man hasn't had the common sense to snatch her off the market by now."

Bridger's mouth curved. "Good sense may not be as common as you suppose."

"You are impossible." She threw up her hands. "And here I believed I raised smart children."

"Working on it, Mom. Give me a chance." He hugged her. "I've done the best I could this summer while twin wrangling and policing Truelove."

She wagged her finger. "Summer leads to autumn. Don't let time slip away from you, son."

"I'm on it, Mom." He gently nudged her with his shoulder. "I have a feeling it's going to be a wonderful fall for all of us."

Austin shouted that Tom had arrived. It was organized chaos for the next few minutes until Bridger got them out the door. Only then did he have a chance to get ready himself.

He was excited and nervous at the same time. He was at the stage in his life where he wasn't interested in casual dating. And with the boys to parent, even more so.

Maggie was the marrying kind. Like him, she was a forthright, straightforward sort of person. One of the things he most admired about her.

He wanted to pursue a serious relationship with her, and he fully intended to tell her so. Tonight? Or would that scare her off him?

Bridger raked his hand over his head. He had to stop second-guessing himself. There was no need to be a nervous wreck. This wasn't just any girl. This was Maggie.

Exactly... He groaned. Which meant he couldn't afford to mess this up.

He took a breath. They were good together. She already loved the twins. The trick would be convincing her to be as fond of him as she was of his two-year-olds.

Bridger shook himself. She was easy to talk to. She was easy to be with. He could be himself around her.

He felt at home. His breath hitched. Because when he was with Maggie, he'd found his home.

Exhaling, he headed toward his bedroom to change clothes. Tonight was the first step toward a new beginning. And he couldn't wait.

Chapter Twelve

Bridger found himself ready far sooner than he anticipated.

Surveying the living room, he scowled. Maggie did her best to keep the house tidy. She required the twins to pick up after themselves before rest time and again before she left each evening. But on the weekends, he wasn't as disciplined with the boys.

Needing to occupy himself until it was time to head to Maggie's, he decided to straighten the house so his mother wouldn't have to when she and Tom returned with the boys.

Tackling the kitchen first, he washed the dishes and wiped off the countertops. Reading Maggie's note on the fridge again, he smiled. Love notes? He'd like to think so.

Grinning, he headed into the living room. He retrieved the couch pillows from the carpet from where Austin and Logan had watched Saturday cartoons this morning.

He tossed a few plastic dinosaurs into the toy bin. A picture book lay open on the coffee table. The same book she read to them every day. Obviously, a favorite. Something about a mother's forever love.

Maggie kept them active, but she also made time for quiet snuggles with books. Yet another example of good parenting. Her maternal instincts were strong for a woman with no children of her own. She never ceased to amaze him.

Flipping idly through the pages, he happened upon the handwritten inscription on the inside cover, dated with Austin and Logan's actual birth date.

> *I pray you will both grow into the strong, good men God created you to be.*
> *Be happy, my sweet boys.*
> *Know I love you always,*
> *Your Mother.*

How Dana and Jeff had loved the twins. This note from Dana was something they could treasure forever. With God's help, he hoped to be the father Austin and Logan needed.

Spotting a juice glass, he closed the book and sighed. He probably should've scouted the house before he started the dishwasher.

Intending to return the book to the shelf in the twins' room, he stuck the book under his arm. But first, he carried the glass into the kitchen and set it beside the sink.

Because he couldn't help himself, he stopped once more in front of the refrigerator to read her note. The notes made him happy. He smiled. Maggie made him happy.

Yet scanning the note, something niggled at the edges of his mind. The handwriting seemed familiar.

His smile faded as his eyes landed on the signature *M* at the bottom of the note.

The signature *M* with which she ended every note. A distinctive capital *M* with flourishes. He frowned. Where had he—

Gasping, he drew the picture book out from underneath his arm. Opening the book, he held the inscription from Dana side by side with the note on the fridge.

His heart thundered. The *M*s were a perfect match. Except the inscription couldn't have been written by his sister-in-law.

Blinking, he shook his head to clear his vision. To make sure. But there was no ignoring the evidence.

Maggie had written the note on the fridge. And she'd also written the inscription in the boys' book. Dated on the occasion of their birth.

Blood roared in his ears. How could this be?

Your Mother...

He stared unseeing out the window overlooking the yard. This had to be a mistake. It couldn't be true.

But he was left with only one possible explanation. One inescapable conclusion.

Maggie was Austin and Logan's birth mother.

The job in Atlanta she'd listed on her résumé. The dates would've coincided with the time of their birth.

Knees suddenly weak, he fell against the counter. In that instant, everything he'd believed about her, about himself, about them, disintegrated to ashes at his feet.

A fierce, stabbing pain pierced his heart. Ribs aching, his head felt near to exploding.

His mother would be devastated. *He* was devastated. The shiny new future he'd allowed himself to believe in was nothing but a lie.

She'd betrayed his trust. He wanted to believe her so badly he'd ignored his gut. Overlooked the twinges of warning.

Little things she'd said and done that didn't make sense at the time now came into the sharp focus of clarity.

In hindsight, there were so many red-flag moments where he'd intended to question her, to prod her for answers. But instead he'd allowed himself to be deflected and distracted. Allowed his senses to become dulled by her big brown eyes. His head turned by a pretty face.

He'd quashed the doubts deep within himself. She'd preyed upon his feelings for her. And he acted as a willing accomplice. Spurning his training, he'd buried his instincts, rather than examining his reservations in the revealing light of objectivity.

Scalding anger like lava burned through his veins.

But Maggie had made a huge error in judgment when she set out to take advantage of him.

He owed it to his brother and Dana to keep the boys safe from the likes of her. An untrustworthy, scheming manipulator.

No matter what it cost him—his job, friends or home—he'd make sure she never hurt his family again.

At the pounding on the door, she hurried down the hall to the living room. Her mouth curved. Like her, perhaps he couldn't wait for their date.

Grabbing the handle, she flung open the door. "Right on ti—"

The instant she saw his face, she realized he knew the truth. The smile died on her lips. His posture was rigid, and his eyes were taut with a cold, implacable anger. He looked at her as if he hated her.

"You're Austin and Logan's biological mother."

She swallowed with difficulty. "Who told you?"

He thrust the book that she'd given the boys at her. "It sure wasn't you."

Stuck to the cover was the note she'd written to him this morning.

He glared. "The inscription signed *'Mother'* isn't Dana's writing. I sent my mother a photo to verify."

Stunned, Maggie stepped back a pace.

His features twisted into someone she didn't recognize. The hard cynicism of a man who dealt with the worst of human nature on a daily basis. "Mom confirmed this is the book their *biological mother* requested be given to them."

"For when the boys were old enough to ask about their first mother." She put a shaky hand to her throat. "When I started taking care of the twins and found the book on their shelf, I realized Dana and Jeff had already given it to them."

"Dana was generous that way." His face shadowed. "Loved those boys more than life itself. Obviously."

"But how did you—"

He tapped his finger against the note sticking to the front cover. "The *M*s."

She swayed.

"Were you ever going to tell me the truth?"

"I wanted to so many times, but I didn't know what to say or how to begin." She took a step forward. "The night we bought shoes with the boys, I tried. But you had such harsh feelings about their birth mother."

Bridger folded his arms across his chest. "I don't

know what I find hardest to forgive—how you continued to deceive us, or that I let you inside in the first place." He scowled. "You. This town. I've lost my edge. The edge that should've seen you coming."

Her stomach convulsed. "I never meant to hurt anyone. Especially not you." Her voice softened.

"Yet you lied to me for weeks." His mouth thinned. "What was it you hoped to gain by insinuating yourself in our affections? What was your endgame? Money?"

"No!" She threw out her hands. "I only wanted a chance to know them."

"Did this devoted-friend role you've been playing provide a sort of sick satisfaction at being able to deceive and manipulate us?"

"It wasn't that way at all." How could she make him understand? "I didn't realize the truth at first. It was only after I became their caregiver, I accidentally discovered the connection. You must believe me."

He curled his lip. "At this point, I don't have to believe anything that comes out of your mouth."

She flinched. "It was only when I learned your last name was the same as the couple I selected, I realized Austin and Logan were my sons."

"DNA does not make them your sons," he growled. "A lesson, strangely enough, I learned from you." Bitterness laced his voice.

"I'm sorry I didn't tell you right away, but I didn't know anything about you. I had to make sure you'd do right by them. Any parent would've done the same."

Bridger's nostrils flared. "A woman who discards her children like nuisances has no right to call herself a parent."

Her entire body trembled. "I never considered them

nuisances. I wanted the best for them. That's why I chose your brother and sister-in-law to give them the kind of life I wanted for them. The life I was unable to give them."

Bridger's mouth flattened. "The aggrieved-mother tactic isn't going to work."

She knotted her hands. "I've grieved for them every day since I gave them up for adoption."

He jabbed his finger in the air between them. "You walked away without a backward glance from the consequences of your selfish irresponsibility."

She stiffened. "That's not fair."

He widened his stance. "Were you coerced into giving them up?"

"No," she said in a small voice.

"Did you, or did you not, willingly enter into an adoption agreement with my brother and Dana?"

She dropped her gaze. "I did."

"Which means you forever relinquished any right to be in their lives." His eyes flashed. "I know because when I uncovered your charade this afternoon, I got out the adoption papers and read them myself."

"You don't know what happened. What led to the most difficult decision of my life. You don't understand the circum—"

"Tell me, then, Maggie." He raked his hand through his hair. "Help me understand."

In his brilliant blue eyes, she beheld pleading. As if he wanted her to say something—anything—to explain her actions of the last few months. To offer an excusable rationale for the inexcusable.

The final awful truth hovered on the tip of her

tongue. She almost told him. But at the last moment, she bit back the words.

She quaked inside, imagining the shock on his face if she told him the rest. The pity. Worse than that, the shame he'd feel on her behalf.

And that was the one thing she didn't think she could bear—seeing the disgust on the face of the man she loved.

She bit back a sob. Yes, she could finally admit it now. She loved Bridger Hollingsworth.

Maybe since the moment he cradled her sons in his arms. Comforting them in the midst of their fears as a thunderstorm raged.

Furthermore, Austin and Logan must never know the truth. The circumstances of their conception would overshadow their lives. She would never allow them to suffer the crippling self-doubt she'd felt since the attack. Therefore, no one else—including the man she loved more than life itself—must ever know, either. Her children had to come first, even at the cost of her own happiness.

Clutching the book to her chest, she lifted her chin. "I—I can't explain."

"You mean you *won't*." His eyes glinted—whatever softness she'd glimpsed, or imagined, wiped clean. "You've left me no choice but to assume the worst. That you've got an ulterior motive that prompted you to embed yourself into our lives."

"Bridger—"

"I'll fight you with every weapon at my disposal. I won't let you take them away from me or my mother. Austin and Logan are Hollingsworths. They belong with us."

"I know," she whispered.

But he went on as if she hadn't spoken.

"I've contacted my attorney. I'm filing for an emergency no-contact order to prevent you from seeing or speaking to any member of my family."

"Bridger, please." She opened her hands. "That won't be—"

"Violating this restraining order will result in your arrest and incarceration." He jutted his jaw. "I don't care who your father, or your family, is in this county. Do I make myself clear?"

Not trusting herself to speak, she nodded.

"Until I can find employment as far away from you as possible, I don't want you within ten feet of a Hollingsworth."

Her heart wrenched. "Wait. You don't have to move away. We can work this out. I don't intend to file for—"

"You are just like Chelsea," he sneered. "And I don't ever want to see you again."

He stalked down the steps toward his truck. Throwing himself inside, he slammed the cab door behind him. The truck rocked.

Engine roaring to life, he sped down the driveway, gravel spraying beneath the tires.

Vision blurring, she staggered onto the porch. Falling over the threshold, she caught hold of the doorframe, only just managing to not land flat on her face. She made it only a few feet before she collapsed into the porch swing.

Covering her face with her hands, tears ran between her fingers. He'd never forgive her, much less trust her again.

The beautiful dream of a future between them was

over. She'd lost him. She'd lost Austin and Logan. She'd lost everything she ever wanted. And she had only herself to blame.

If only she'd told him the truth at the beginning. Instead of trusting God to work good for all of them, she'd chosen to trust herself. To try to control the situation for the outcome she wanted.

"Oh, God," she sobbed. "I'm so sorry. Forgive me."

Pain seared her. Alongside hurt and confusion and sadness. Like the day she handed the twins into the arms of the social workers.

Worse. Because she hadn't truly known those tiny bundles of baby joy. This time she knew what she was losing.

Her funny, sunny Austin. Her still-waters-ran-deep Logan. Yet not hers. She took a ragged breath. They'd never been and would never be hers.

She wasn't sure how long she sat there, inconsolably weeping. As alone, but for God, as she'd ever been since that life-changing night.

In the drive, an engine sounded. She could tell without looking it wasn't Bridger. A door clicked shut softly. Gravel crunched. The steps creaked. Her father dropped onto the swing beside her, and she raised her head.

"Wilda got a text from Bridger. Upset, she insisted we return to her house."

Maggie put her fist against her mouth. "She didn't tell you?"

"No, she didn't." He rested his shoulder blades against the slats in the swing. "Is this about your sons, Maggie?"

She sucked in a breath. "You know about Austin and Logan?"

"Not at first." His gaze filled with love. "But Austin's

ear infection reminded me of how sick you used to get as a little girl. And that set me to thinking. Logan bears a strong resemblance to the wee Magpie I remember so well." Her father sighed. "And once upon a time, the less gray, younger version of myself. As for Austin…"

"Mom," she whispered.

A faint smile curved his thin lips. "She would've loved them so much."

Sadness consumed Maggie. "I love them so much, Dad."

"I take it Bridger didn't respond as you hoped when you told him the truth."

She knotted her hands in her lap. "I didn't get the chance to tell him. I planned to, but—"

Her father winced. "He found out first. Not good, I'm guessing."

"It's such a tangled mess, Dad. He's contacted an attorney. Forbidding me to see them."

Her father straightened. "They are your children. After a life in law enforcement, I don't have a large retirement account, but it's yours, Magpie. We'll fight for custody, if that's what you want to do."

"Oh, Dad." Tears welled in her eyes. "After losing their parents, how can I take them away from the only other people they've ever loved?"

"They love you, too, Maggie. I've seen it on their little faces. The way they look at you. The way they interact with you. You're their mother, and you deserve the chance to know them."

She hugged her father.

His shoulders sagged. "We lost your mom too soon. There is so much I would do differently if I had the chance. I'm so sorry you felt you couldn't come to me when you found yourself pregnant. Perhaps if I'd been a better dad you would've never given them—"

"No, Dad." She squeezed his hand. "None of this is your fault. I was too ashamed to tell you the truth. I couldn't bear knowing I'd disappointed you."

He shook his head. "Nothing you could ever do, or not do, would ever stop me from loving you. If Austin or Logan were in trouble, you'd love them no matter what. Somehow I failed to communicate that to you." He laid his rough palm on her cheek. "Forgive me, Magpie, please."

After getting to know her boys, she realized what her father said was true. Her love for the twins was fierce and nonnegotiable.

She'd always battled the need to prove herself sufficient and independent. It was only when she'd found herself alone and pregnant that she'd finally turned to God, the only all-sufficient one. She should've trusted her father, too.

"There's nothing to forgive, Dad. Your work was important. You were, and still are, my hero. Always."

His chin wobbled. "But if—"

"No what-ifs. I have to believe despite the pain, God is in control." She bit her lip. "Back then, I prayed for guidance about what to do. I felt God leading me to Jeff and Dana Hollingsworth." She lifted her hands and dropped them. "But how everything that's happened since fits into His plan, I don't know."

Her father exhaled. "That's when faith is most important. When we don't have the answers."

She sighed. "And yet we choose to trust anyway."

His Adam's apple bobbed in his throat. "I hate to

bring this up, but I have to ask if the twins' father might also come into play."

She'd done everything in her power to avoid telling him what happened that terrible night three years ago. Now she understood what it felt like to be a parent, she knew this part of the story would cause her father an enormous amount of anguish.

"I was stupid, Dad. You taught me to be alert and vigilant. To listen to my instincts. To not become a victim. To keep myself safe, but…"

"Safe?" His eyes widened. "Maggie…"

"Part of my job at the firm was to take care of out-of-town clients. Escort them from the hotel to meetings. Arrange dinners."

Her chest heaved. Nausea roiled in her belly.

If she was going to get this out, she had to do it fast, or she'd never find the courage to do it at all.

"He was the spoiled son of our biggest account. He flirted with me the entire week. Ignoring my instincts for the sake of the big deal, I tried to be friendly. But he pushed it further than I was comfortable."

She was having trouble drawing a full breath. "He— he wouldn't take no for an answer."

She gripped her dad's calloused palm, grateful for his strength. "I was so ashamed, Daddy."

Her father's face had gone white. "You were the victim of a crime." He clenched and unclenched his fists. "Tell me he's rotting in prison somewhere."

She let out a shaky sigh.

"I went to the nearest police station." She gulped. "I couldn't let him hurt someone else. Humiliate someone else…"

"He was a predator, Maggie."

"I was waiting in the reception area to file a complaint with an officer. But playing on the television, there was a breaking news story about a fiery vehicular collision in the early-morning commuter traffic on the freeway."

Her father's jaw tightened.

"The driver made the news because his family was so important. He lost control of his expensive sports car. He died at the scene."

"Couldn't have happened to a nicer person," her father grunted.

"I realized he'd never hurt me or anyone else again. So I left without seeing an officer." She lowered her gaze. "Three weeks later, I discovered I was pregnant," she whispered.

Her father made a choked sound. She looked up. Fist to his mouth, tears streamed across her dad's grizzled cheeks.

Except at her mother's funeral, she'd never seen her dad shed any tears. She felt the stark helplessness of seeing someone you loved suffer and being unable to assuage the pain.

A racking grief engulfed her dad. "You thought because you were a police chief's daughter, you'd let me down? Oh, Maggie, baby." His shoulders shook. "I'm so sorry, honey. So sorry this happened to you."

This time it was Maggie who put her arms around him. And they cried together.

She cupped his face between her hands. "'But as for me, I know that my redeemer liveth…'"

His eyes awash with more unshed tears, he nodded. "'…And at the latter day, he shall stand upon the earth.'"

The verse from the book of Job was her father's refuge against the evil and injustice he'd witnessed in his career. His personal statement of faith, no matter what.

Because in the end, that was what faith was all about—the no-matter-whats.

"I love you, Dad."

"We're going to get through this, Magpie." He held her close. "You and me. You're not going to walk through this alone."

A truth she'd discovered three years ago, rain did fall upon both the just and the unjust. But even so, there was a difference. Though broken and battered, she'd been held in the palm of God's hand. She'd never been alone. And as His child, she never would be.

No matter what.

Chapter Thirteen

Over the next few days, Bridger was as good as his word. He cut Maggie off from Austin and Logan. The last week of the Tumbling Tots session, they were a no-show.

She was glad for classes to end. And yet, staying busy would have been a welcome distraction. Though nothing could compensate for the hollowness she felt inside.

The twins had to wonder where she was. They must be asking for her. Did they cry for her?

In the dark of night, she cried for them. The idea they might believe she abandoned them—again—gutted her.

She found it impossible to sleep. To eat. To do anything but mourn the loss of her children. And she didn't just grieve for the boys. She ached for the future she'd never share with Bridger.

If she'd been honest when she first uncovered her connection with the boys, maybe this terrible outcome could have been avoided. Yet from the moment she decided to hide her real identity, this consequence had been inevitable.

Despite what he believed about her, for months she'd waged an internal war with the desire to tell the truth. But she'd delayed and procrastinated doing what she knew to be right. Hesitation had proved fatal to all her hopes and dreams.

She couldn't shake the look in his eyes when he'd confronted her with the truth—the anger, the disappointment, but worst of all, the horrible sense of betrayal.

If only she'd come to him and Wilda. Yet it was better he believe her a lying manipulator than he learn the ugly truth about the conception of Austin and Logan. Whatever it cost her, she must protect them. And to ensure their well-being, there was one further thing she must do.

Yanking the clothes off the hangers in her closet, she tossed them onto the bed.

"Please don't do this, Mary Margaret." GeorgeAnne hunched her shoulders. "It doesn't have to end this way."

Folding a blouse, she placed it in her suitcase. "I think it does have to end this way, Aunt G."

Her aunt shook her bony finger. "Just so you know, Bridger's mother is not pleased with how he's handling the situation."

A small portion of her anguish eased at this news. She admired and loved his mom. With her subterfuge revealed, she'd hated to contemplate what Wilda must think of her.

"I'd hoped your father would've talked some sense into you."

She folded another shirt. "The Hollingsworths have endured enough tragedy. I won't drag them into a lengthy court battle. Austin and Logan have begun to settle into their new home. They're happy in Truelove. I refuse to subject them to more trauma and upheaval."

GeorgeAnne flung out her hands. "But what about you? What about the trauma you suffered? What about upending your own life? Leaving your family and friends?"

Hot tears prickled her eyelids. "It doesn't matter about me."

"It does matter about you."

"I—I can't alter the circumstances of their birth. But this one thing I can do. They must never know." She caught hold of GeorgeAnne's liver-spotted hand. "Promise me, Aunt G. I want them to be happy."

GeorgeAnne touched her cheek. "What makes every child most happy is to be with their mother, honey."

A deep well of sadness opened inside Maggie. "I love my children too much to fight over them. With me gone, Bridger can be happy here, too."

One day, he'd meet someone worthy of his trust. Someone who'd make a more fitting mother for Austin and Logan. Someone who'd be a loving support to the police chief.

With all her heart, she longed to be that person for him. If only he'd given her a chance. But she'd run out of chances.

GeorgeAnne sank onto the mattress. "Where will you go?"

For the first time in Maggie's memory, her great-aunt looked every bit of her seventy-plus years. Maggie was so very, very sorry about that, too.

"An old friend—she and her husband own a recreational water sports business—put me in contact with a parks and rec director looking to fill a vacant position in Virginia Beach."

GeorgeAnne pressed her lips together. "Virginia Beach?" She sounded on the verge of tears.

Her heart skipped a beat. If never-say-die Aunt G started crying, she wasn't sure she could stand it. She was holding herself together only by a thread.

"Dad or I will call to let you know we arrived safely."

GeorgeAnne's mouth quivered. "I'm glad your father is helping you find a new place."

She was glad, too. Glad not to have to apartment hunt by herself. Glad not to have to face saying goodbye to her hometown alone. Watching the where-true-love-awaits sign slowly disappear in her rearview mirror.

Her true love *would* wait in Truelove. But he wasn't awaiting her. She shook herself. No point in dwelling on what might have been.

"Dad will insist on alerting any long-lost buddies on the Virginia Beach police force to keep an eye out for me. It'll be all I can do to persuade him to leave me there."

"If he decides to stay—" GeorgeAnne lifted her chin "—good for him. But I'd like to smack our new police chief upside his thick skull."

She stilled. "Don't make this worse, Aunt G. Some broken things are never meant to be fixed."

"But some things are." GeorgeAnne rose. "And at my age, I think I've lived long enough and gained the wisdom necessary to know the difference."

"Aunt—"

GeorgeAnne waved her hand. "When do you intend to leave?"

"This afternoon." A band of sorrow tightened around

her chest, making it difficult to breathe. "It's too late for me and Bridger, Aunt G."

"While the Double Name Club has life and breath, it's never too late, Mary Margaret." Her aunt's steel blue eyes glinted. "You're letting your fears control you."

"No," she whispered. "This time, I'm letting love control me."

But the man she loved with every fiber of her being didn't love her. And before she lost her nerve, she had to do the hardest thing of all—walk away from her beloved children.

Again.

It had been a bad week.

Since the confrontation with Maggie on Saturday, a perpetual headache had dogged Bridger.

Unable to concentrate, he shuffled through the papers on his desk at the station. He'd begun writing his resignation letter, but gotten stuck. He hated to leave the department shorthanded, yet under the circumstances…

He rubbed his throbbing temples, willing the pain to subside. He knew better than to expect the jagged pain in his heart to subside anytime soon. Recalling the angry scene with Maggie, regret sliced through him for the hurt his words had inflicted.

In the darkest hours of the night when he lay sleepless, staring at the ceiling above his bed, the memory of her stricken face haunted him.

Doubt warred with his anger over her deceit. A justifiable anger. She'd lied to them.

Yet he couldn't shake his misgivings. Had he been wrong? Had he jumped to the wrong conclusions?

He gave her the opportunity to explain, but she shut

down on him. And despite everything, thoughts of her continued to consume him.

Bridger scrubbed his face. If only her image was as easily erased. Maggie had become a bad habit he couldn't seem to break.

Try as he might to stoke the anger inside him, happier times flitted relentlessly through his mind.

Her radiant face helping the boys blow out their birthday candles. Her feminine squeal after he'd drenched her with the water hose. Her laughing revenge when she'd chased him down and turned the hose on him.

Just when he'd begun to think—to hope—there might be a future for him with Maggie—

He shoved back his chair, the legs scraping like fingernails on a chalkboard across the linoleum.

Stupid, futile speculations. Dulling his indignation. Filling him with sadness for what was never meant to be. Encumbering him with an unrequited longing for the Maggie who'd only ever existed in his imagination.

A commotion sounded in the hallway outside his office. He was rounding the desk to investigate when GeorgeAnne stormed inside.

"You've got a lot to answer for, Chief Hollingsworth." She planted her hands on her hips. "And I'm here to set you straight."

He bristled. "Miss GeorgeAnne…" With effort, he drew together the tattered remnants of his patience. "You need to calm d—"

"Don't you dare tell me to calm down, young man." Behind the horn-rimmed glasses, her eyes blazed. If looks could kill, he reckoned he'd already be dead where he stood. "Not after the way you've behaved."

"The way *I've* behaved?" he growled. "What Maggie did was indefensible."

"You can get right off that high horse you're riding, Bridger Hollingsworth."

He rubbed the back of his neck. "I think you should leave before we say things we can't take back."

"That pride of yours will be your undoing. And you'd do well to let it go before you lose the best thing, other than the twins, to ever come into your life."

"You can't lose something you never had, Miss GeorgeAnne." His nostrils flared. "She lied to me. About everything."

GeorgeAnne set her jaw. "Not about everything. Not about how she feels about the boys. About you."

"She lied to me, most of all." He laughed, more of a mirthless bark than genuine amusement. "Besides, it doesn't matter now. It's over."

The old lady shook her head. "It doesn't have to be over. There is a way forward. If you're half the man Maggie believes you to be, you'll find the path to her."

He glared. "There is no coming back from what Maggie did."

GeorgeAnne's eyes bored into him. "Try the road called forgiveness and compassion."

Sharp agony needled his chest. "What does it matter?" He jammed his hands into his uniform pockets. "We were never going to work. It wasn't real."

"I don't believe that. I saw the way she looked at you. And how you looked at her. The two of you are worth fighting for." She pushed up her sleeves. "Even if you're both too pigheaded to fight for yourselves."

Closing his eyes, he pinched the bridge of his nose.

"What I feel, or don't feel, has nothing to do with keeping her relationship to the twins secret."

"She was afraid."

He opened his eyes.

"Rightfully so, considering how you reacted." GeorgeAnne opened her palms. "She loves those children. She'd never do anything to hurt them. You've seen how she is with them."

"An act." His mouth twisted. "Whatever she did for them in the present doesn't erase her desertion of them in the past."

GeorgeAnne crossed her arms. "The past is exactly why I've come to talk to you."

He widened his stance. "I'm not sure what you hope to accomplish, Miss GeorgeAnne. Your misguided loyalty to Maggie—"

"I didn't know about her true relationship with the twins until recently. No one did. She didn't even tell her father."

He stared at her for a moment. Some of the distress he'd felt eased. It had pained him to think GeorgeAnne and Tom—the whole town—had conspired against him.

Bridger took a ragged breath. "There's nothing you can say that will change my mind about your niece's unfitness to be anywhere near my boys. If you're angling for shared custody, you're wasting your breath."

"Keeping Austin and Logan from her is destroying Maggie, Bridger." GeorgeAnne squared her shoulders. "That's why I'm here. To tell you the last bit of truth she's unable to tell you herself. Because she's got a mistaken notion about protecting the twins. And because she can't bear to speak the words to you."

He scowled. "What're you talking about?"

"Three years ago, Maggie was assaulted."

The air left his lungs in a whoosh.

Suddenly weak, he leaned heavily against the edge of his desk. Not Maggie. It couldn't be true.

"After discovering she was pregnant, she made the courageous decision to distance herself from the twins. So they might enjoy a life untainted with the knowledge they were the result of an assault."

Bits and pieces of conversations flitted through his mind. Things she'd shared. Let slip about herself.

He'd believed she endured an abusive relationship with a previous boyfriend. She'd let him believe that. But she'd endured so much more than what he'd supposed.

Bridger struggled to wrap his mind around the horror of what had happened to her. His tough, funny, beautiful Maggie.

"Why did she refuse to explain?" he rasped.

"She doesn't want Austin and Logan to ever learn the truth."

He raked his hand over his head. "Why didn't she trust me?"

"Since the attack, she has a hard time trusting men. But that first day when I witnessed how she responded to you—how you were with her—" GeorgeAnne's eyes glistened. "I hoped. Oh, how I hoped."

Maggie's initial skittishness made sense now. How startled she'd been by his touch. Any touch. The two-steps-forward, one-step-backward dance he'd felt between them.

"She's so caught up in the shame of what happened and so sure of your rejection, she couldn't bear for you to know," GeorgeAnne whispered.

Head in his hands, he groaned. Shame engulfed him.

His own fears had gotten the better of him. He should've trusted her. And God.

"I've ruined everything. She'll never forgive me for how I treated her. For what I said."

GeorgeAnne put her hand on his shoulder. "I think you'll find Mary Margaret has a great deal of experience with forgiveness." She became brisk. "Tomorrow will be too late, though. You must hurry before you lose your chance with her."

He raised his head. "What's going on?"

"She doesn't want you to lose the life you've built here in town."

He straightened. "What do you mean?"

"Funny thing about love, isn't it?" A small smile lifted the old lady's wrinkled lips. "She loves you and the twins so much, she's willing to do the leaving for you."

His lungs constricted. Maggie was leaving? She needed her friends. Her family. Her home.

Bridger couldn't let her make this supreme self-sacrifice. He swallowed. Not again.

He could no longer deny his feelings for her. He and the boys needed her in their lives as much as she needed them. For always and forever.

Bridger was desperately in love with Maggie. He would grovel, beg her forgiveness, do anything to keep from losing her. Austin and Logan needed their mother.

The strongest, most wonderful woman he'd ever known.

And it was high time he told her so.

Closing the trunk of her car, Maggie took a final look at the purple-blue haze on the surrounding mountain ridge. The job in Virginia Beach would offer a far different view.

She wasn't sure when—if ever—she'd live here again. But this town, this place, would always be her home. And though she might never return, this was where her heart would permanently reside.

At the sound of tires, she looked up and saw Bridger's cruiser headed up the driveway. She tensed, fearing another confrontation, and yet filled with the desire to see him one more time. Her dad came out onto the porch.

Bridger unfolded from the cruiser.

Her father stalked down the steps. "What do you want, Hollingsworth?"

She frowned. "Dad."

"He's got a right to be angry with me." Bridger took off his hat. "After the way things went down between us last time."

Clenching his fists, her father inserted himself between her and Bridger. "If you're here to serve the restraining order, you've wasted your time."

She took hold of his sleeve. "Daddy."

"I never filed the order." His gaze flicked between her and her father. "I just want to talk to Maggie."

"Absolutely not. You've made yourself perfectly clear." Her father pointed to the road. "Now let me make myself clear. Get off my property."

"Dad!"

Bridger looked at them. "I want to apologize for the things I said. The false assumptions I made."

It was not what either of them had expected. Rocking on his heels, her father cut his eyes to her.

"I should've never spoken to your daughter the way I

did, sir." A muscle pinged in his jaw. "I want to apologize to you for not giving Maggie the respect she deserves."

A silence fell, broken only by the sigh of the wind through the trees.

Her father folded his arms. "Whether or not my daughter wants to talk to you, Hollingsworth, is entirely her decision."

"Dad, it's okay." She tugged his sleeve. "Give us a minute, please?"

"Nothing about this situation is okay. But I'll leave you two to talk." His dark eyes, so very like Logan's, narrowed. "And I'll be inside if you need me to eject an unwelcome guest."

Shoulders stiff, her father strode across the grass and went back into the house.

Maggie waited until the door closed with a click behind him. "I'm sorry. He's—"

"He has every right to be protective." Bridger turned the hat in his hand. "Can't say I wouldn't react the same or worse if someone treated the boys the way I…" A pulse leaped in his throat. "GeorgeAnne came to see me this morning. She told me about Atlanta."

Maggie's breathed hitched. "I didn't want you to ever…" An immense weariness enveloped her. *Aunt G, what have you done?*

Hand on her throat, she turned her gaze away from him toward the horizon.

The look on her face gutted him.

"I'm so sorry about what happened to you."

Suddenly, he didn't know what to do with his hands. He wanted so badly to take her into his arms. But he didn't have the right. And he never wanted to do anything to make her feel afraid or uncomfortable.

"Please, look at me, Maggie." His voice choked. "I know you must hate me."

"I don't hate you," she whispered.

"You're nothing like Chelsea. I was so wrong."

She faced him, fear and confusion written across her features. "I deserved everything you said."

"You didn't deserve what I said, or what happened to you." He hated himself for the fear he'd put in her eyes. "I don't deserve your forgiveness. But if you could find it in your heart to ever—"

"I forgive you, Bridger." She wrapped her arms around herself. "But I—I can't stay in Truelove."

"Don't leave town. Please. Austin and Logan need their mother. They need you." His voice dropped low in his throat. "I—I need you."

"If you tell them who I am, eventually they'll have questions." Her mouth trembled. "Answers I never want them to know. A burden I don't want them to shoulder."

Placing his hat on the cruiser, he took a step forward, watching her face for any flicker of discomfort.

"Having their mother outweighs any other consideration. Your love will allow them to thrive, so one day when they're old enough to know the truth, the past will have less power to harm them."

A breeze ruffled her hair. "I—I'm not sure how we go from here."

"We trust God to lead us." He took another step forward. "We can work out the details. I'm committed to the twins being part of your life." He swallowed. "I want to be a part of your life, too."

She bit her lip. His heart plummeted.

"It's hard for you to trust men. I get that." He took a breath. "But I promise I'm going to do everything in my power to earn your trust again. To be the man you deserve."

Tears made a slow trek down her cheeks.

He longed with everything inside him to wipe her tears away but he dared not. Not unless she gave him permission to touch her again.

"Bridger, I'm not sure…" She looked away again.

"We'll walk through this together. You're not alone anymore. I'll be by your side. As long as you want me to be."

She tucked a tendril of hair behind her ear.

"You set the pace. I won't rush you." He searched her face. "I'm leaving it to you to tell me when you feel ready to be more than friends. Would that be okay?"

She nodded. "But you shouldn't have to wait for me to get my emotions together."

"You're my true love, Maggie." His gaze met hers. "And you are worth waiting for."

Chapter Fourteen

Six months ago, Maggie would never have believed it possible to be this happy.

The boys divided their time between Bridger's house and hers. She and her dad had fixed a bedroom for the twins when they spent the night, which they did often.

With her by his side, Bridger told the boys she was their mother. Despite her fears, Austin and Logan accepted her relationship to them without question. Children were far more resilient than she'd given them credit for, and they'd thrived on the changes in their lives.

Every time they called her Mommy, another piece of her heart healed. She reckoned she'd never tire of hearing the sweet endearment from their lips.

Grandpa Tom became their favorite fishing buddy. Grandma Wilda remained their favorite cookie maker. Maggie found herself embraced by Bridger's sister and her family, too.

Together, she and Bridger told their closest friends the truth. She left it to the savvy wisdom of the matchmakers to inform the rest of Truelove. Stepping into her new role as Austin and Logan's mother, she felt only love and support from the community.

With the changes in her life, she resumed therapy with a local counselor. At her request, Bridger attended a few sessions with her, so he might better understand the emotional obstacles she faced. He proved nothing short of wonderful in his efforts to reassure her of how beautiful she was to him.

He already knew the bare bones of what happened to her, but she found the courage to tell him the rest of her story. He made her feel safe. Safe enough to share the darkest chapter of her life.

When she told him about that night in Atlanta, this strong, wonderful man, whom she loved more than life itself, wept at the sorrow she'd endured. And she loved him all the more for how cherished he made her feel.

The light in her life far outshone the darkness. At long last, she felt herself emerging from the stranglehold of the lies she'd believed about herself. Finally, the peace that had eluded her felt within reach.

She and Bridger gradually increased the twins' time with her. Now they spent only weekends at Bridger's house. But they saw plenty of him during the week. He stopped by the rec center for lunch most days after her classes. More often than not, he ate dinner with her, the boys and her dad.

Harvest season was in full swing for the orchard growers in the valley. The mornings began now with a brisk, apple-crisp chill. The vivid orange, red and yellow riot of the Blue Ridge autumn foliage would soon be at a glorious peak.

Wilda bought a bungalow on the same street where ErmaJean Hicks lived. Maggie hadn't failed to notice how her dad continued to drop by to make sure Wilda was getting settled. And from the gleam in Aunt G's eye, Maggie wasn't the only one to notice.

One early-October evening after the dinner dishes were washed and the boys put to bed, out on the swing, she mentioned as much to Bridger. There wouldn't be many more evenings like this. Once darkness fell, the nights grew cool.

She ran her gaze over the angular line of his jaw. "Do you mind?"

He smiled, the tiny lines at the corner of his eyes lifted. Her heart hitched. That crazy butterfly tango went off in her midsection.

The exhilarating effect he had on her nerve endings hadn't abated since the first day he looked at her. And she hoped it never would.

He draped his arm across her shoulders. "It has been my personal experience that the matchmakers might be smarter than the rest of us combined."

She'd made another less pleasing discovery in recent days, too. A deep insecurity had him believing it was only because of the twins she kept him in her life. Probably the result of the number his previous girlfriend had done on his head. *Thanks for nothing, Chelsea.*

Getting out of the swing, he offered her his hand. "I'll be out of town for a few days at a law enforcement conference. But I'll talk to the boys every night before they go to bed."

They walked to the steps together.

She lifted her face, waiting and hoping he would kiss her. He kissed her cheek instead. A man of his word, he'd meant what he said about taking their relationship slow. She let out a breath of disappointment. Perhaps too slow.

Her heart ached as he drove away alone. Without her and the boys. She sighed. There was such a thing, she was discovering, as too much patience.

Bridger called every night to pray good-night prayers over the phone with the twins. And while her dad finished putting the boys to bed, he'd stay on the line with her. They talked and laughed until Bridger finally called it a night.

"I've got a workshop to lead tomorrow."

Sometimes when he had a break between presentations, he'd text her a funny little quote, or a thinking-of-you emoji. Her thoughts were filled with him.

Every night with increasing reluctance, she let him go. When he was asked to consult on a cold case he'd worked while with the Raleigh Police Department, the few days of absence turned into a week.

His phone call was the highlight of her day. At the sound of his voice, her heart went into overdrive. She became impatient for his return.

"I think we can wrap up the case by Saturday at the latest," he told her when she pressed him. "I should be home by Sunday."

Home. She loved the sound of the word on his lips. Only problem, it was Thursday night. Sunday seemed very far away.

Friday morning, GeorgeAnne arrived to take the boys on an outing to a farm outside town. Maggie sent Austin and Logan to put on their jackets. She and her aunt transferred the car seats to her aunt's truck.

She gave the seats a tug to make sure they were secure. "Are you sure you want to tackle the corn maze with Austin and Logan?"

"I raised five rambunctious boys." GeorgeAnne gave her a quelling look. "I think I can handle your two."

She pulled on the ends of her ponytail. "Maybe I should go with you."

"Every mother deserves time to relax. And I'm looking forward to spending time with my double great-nephews." GeorgeAnne shrugged. "Besides, Tom and Wilda are meeting us there."

They returned to the porch.

Peering into Maggie's features, GeorgeAnne scrunched her face. "With Chief Hollingsworth due back this weekend, I thought you'd jump at the opportunity to do something to make yourself presentable."

She put her hand on her hip. "Bridger likes me the way I am, Aunt G."

"Of course he does. Nothing wrong with the man's eyes." GeorgeAnne's lips twitched. "But a little paint—"

"Never hurt any old barn." She rolled her eyes. "I know. I know."

GeorgeAnne raised her voice. "If you boys don't get a move on, the Aunt G train is pulling out of the station without you."

There were thuds from within. Maggie winced. Two pairs of feet thundered out the door. The twins barreled toward them. "Aunt G! Aunt G!"

Despite her grumpy, carefully cultivated reputation for tolerating no nonsense, the old lady's eyes lightened at the sight of the boys.

When the twins were buckled into their car seats in her truck, GeorgeAnne handed them each a granola bar. "Something to munch on. Can't have them dying of hunger on my watch."

Blowing kisses, Maggie closed the truck door. But chewing her lip, she lingered.

GeorgeAnne scrolled down the window. "Are you nervous about Bridger coming home, Mary Margaret?"

"I'm so afraid of making a mistake, Aunt G. Of hurting Bridger. Of not being the woman he deserves."

GeorgeAnne squeezed her arm. "Six months ago, you had no idea you'd ever see your sons again, yet here you are. God promises the impossible because nothing is impossible for Him."

"Thank you for always being there for me." Leaning through the open window, she gave the brusque old woman a firm hug. "In case I haven't told you lately, I love you, Aunt G."

"I love you, too." She laid her calloused palm on Maggie's cheek. "Our God is in the hope-creating, future-making business. Trust Him. Trust Bridger. Trust your heart." Fluttering her hand, her aunt became brisk. "But enough of that. We'll see you later."

Maggie waved until the truck disappeared down the driveway. Her sons were happy, safe and secure. Surrounded by friends and family, who loved them devotedly.

After months of constant two-year-old noise, the farmhouse felt strangely quiet and empty without them.

Restless, she threw herself into cleaning the windows. A bucket of water and vinegar at her feet, she was wiping the last window on the front of the house when she heard the sound of tires on gravel.

Back so soon? It wasn't even lunchtime. Laying aside the cloth, she turned.

Her heart lodged in her throat. Bridger's truck pulled up to the house. As he got out, his face transformed at the sight of her on the porch.

Suddenly the fear, the doubts, the uncertainties floated away. For the first time, she beheld as if in a dream the possibility of a life in the farmhouse next door. With the twins. But most of all, with Bridger.

To never have to say good-night and watch him drive away without her ever again. She longed, like a child yearned for Christmas morning, for the joy of quiet moments together. For a lifetime together. To be a family. To be his wife.

And she knew.

She scrambled down the steps.

He raised his hand. "Hey, stranger."

She fast-walked across the lawn.

He shut the cab door. "Case concluded earlier than I thought."

At a run now, she closed the distance between them.

"Drove straight through so I could—"

She threw her arms around him.

Caught off guard, he staggered into the truck. Reflexes kicking in, he put his arms around her, but just as quickly, he let go. "Maggie?"

She buried her face in his shirt. "You're home," she whispered.

His arms went around her again. "With a reception like this—" he rubbed the stubble of his cheek against the crown of her head "—maybe I should leave home more often."

She lifted her gaze to his.

A crease puckered his brow. "It's been a long week with the boys, huh?"

"I've missed you, Bridger Hollingsworth." She took hold of both sides of his face, the stubble scraping her palms. "You have your own place in my heart. A place that has nothing to do with Austin and Logan."

A flickering hope ignited in his eyes.

Oh, those eyes.

"I love you, Bridger. I'm ready. Ready for us to become a family." Tears leaked out of her eyes. "Ready to become your wife. If you want me."

He drew her closer. "I want you. For always and forever, I will cherish you." His lips brushed her forehead. "My life is beautiful because you, Maggie Arledge, are in it."

She cocked her head. "Are you going to kiss me, or stand there talking all day?"

He gave her a slow, devastating smile. "If you want kissing, I think I could arrange that."

And he did.

When GeorgeAnne returned with the twins, Austin and Logan were overjoyed to see him. It did Maggie's heart good to see him play-wrestle with them in the living room. Over the next week, he spent a lot of time with them. Guy time, he told her.

Yet he said nothing else about building a life together. Nor made any moves toward making that dream a reality. She was beginning to feel neglected.

On Saturday morning, he called. "Could the boys spend the day with me? I have a few things I could use their help with."

"I can help, too."

"Nah... I think we can manage without you this time. I'll pick them up soon." He clicked off.

More guy time? She sniffed.

Feeling unnecessary, she frowned at the cell in her hand. When it came to the helpfulness of two-year-olds, Bridger might live to regret not taking her up on her offer.

A few minutes later, he arrived. Got the boys. And left. It was late afternoon when the phone rang again. She glanced at the screen. It was Bridger.

If she had any pride she would've let it ring at least twice. But missing her guys, she snatched it up on the first ring. "H-hello?"

"Maggie? You sound out of breath. Are you okay?"

"Fine," she said. "Everything going well with the twins?"

"If you're not busy, there's something I want to show you," Bridger said.

She straightened. "I'll be right over."

But when she arrived at Bridger's place, she found him raking leaves into a pile.

Austin climbed onto a nearby stump. "Watch me, Mommy."

Bridger leaned on the rake. "I knew you wouldn't want to miss this."

She folded her arms into the warmth of her cardigan. This was why he'd called her to come over?

"Mommy? Awe you watching, Mommy? *Mommy!*"

Shooting a mildly irritated glare in Bridger's direction, she dropped her arms and smiled. "I'm watching, Austin."

He launched himself at the leaves.

Then Logan had to show her, too. Giggling, the boys rolled over and over in the pile.

Bridger laughed. "I think Mommy should jump into the leaves. What do you think, guys?"

"Jump, Mommy!"

"Jump wike me."

She planted her hands on her hips. "This is what y'all have been doing all day?"

"Among other things." Bridger's gaze dropped to the leaf pile. "We took a drive along the parkway into town, too."

A drive along the Blue Ridge Parkway this time of year was nothing short of spectacular. *Not that she'd been invited.*

"Sounds like you had fun."

His mouth quirked. "Now that you're here, though, the real fun begins."

She narrowed her eyes. Was he teasing her?

"Mommy!"

"Jump!"

Bridger offered his hand. As if she needed his assistance to step on top of the twelve-inch-high stump. But she took his hand anyway. And was rewarded when he squeezed her fingers.

Leaning closer, his lips brushed the hair above her ear. She caught a whiff of his aftershave and the pungent aroma of fallen leaves.

"I missed you," he whispered.

Her heart did a dance inside her chest. Stepping on the stump, she missed his hand when he let go.

"Make room," she called to the boys. "I'm going to jump."

It wasn't a very big jump. But stooping a bit, she stepped off the stump, and allowed herself to fall backward into the leaves.

"Hoo-way! Hoo-way!"

"Daddy next!"

He winked at her. "Don't mind if I do." Throwing aside the rake, he pretended to make a mighty leap but landed softly beside her.

Austin and Logan pounced on him at once. She laughed at the blur of limbs and leaves as her guys rolled around in the pile.

"Wait!" He stiffened. "What's that I feel underneath my back?" He fumbled along the ground, rummaging through the leaves beneath him. Lifting his hand, he held up a small black box.

Heart pounding, she sat up.

"What's this?" He widened his eyes. "Do you boys know how this got there?"

Austin and Logan giggled.

Getting off the ground, he took a knee. "The twins have something they'd like to say."

But then, silence. He frowned.

"Guys?" he coaxed.

Austin buried his face in Bridger's jacket. "I forget."

"Boys… Don't leave me hanging here."

She laughed. "Two-year-olds."

He smiled. "Gotta love them." He turned to Logan. "Remember? What we practiced," he whispered.

"I 'member." He opened his pudgy little-boy hands. "Will you marry Daddy, Mommy?"

Her breath caught.

Logan's brown eyes darted to Bridger. "Dat what I 'posed to say, wight?"

Bridger ran his hand over her son's dark head. "That was exactly right."

Logan turned to her. "Mommy?"

Her chin quivered. "Perfect."

"Maggie?" Bridger's gaze fastened onto hers, a question in his eyes. "Was there an answer in there somewhere?"

"Is there something in the box for me?" She plucked a leaf out of her hair. "I wasn't sure if I should direct my answer to Logan or you."

"To me. Definitely me. And yeah." His Adam's apple bobbed. "There's something in the box for you from me." He popped open the box to reveal a stunning emerald-cut diamond.

She swallowed past the lump in her throat.

"Thought I better do this part myself." He shook his head. "I had nightmares about the twins dropping the ring into the leaves and never finding it again."

"So you've been planning this?"

His brows arched. "Well, yeah. I told you how I felt."

She rested her chin on her up-drawn knees. "You might need to tell me again so I don't forget. You might need to tell me every day for the rest of our lives."

Bridger gave her a lopsided smile. "I think that could be arranged. Does that mean your answer is yes? You'll marry me?"

His rugged face, so beloved to her, looked uncertain. And she decided to stop teasing him.

"Yes, I'll marry you."

He grinned. "Woo-hoo! Boys, Mommy says she'll marry us."

"Hoo-way!"

"Yay!"

Austin and Logan hurled themselves at Maggie and Bridger.

"The ring!" she shouted.

He held the box above their heads. "Got it."

She held out her hand. "Better put it on my finger to make sure it's safe, Chief."

Growing bored, the boys ran off to investigate a moth clinging to the trunk of a tree.

Taking advantage of the lull, Bridger slid the ring onto her finger. "I love you, Maggie."

She gave a little shiver of pleasure. "I love you, too."

"Mommy! Daddy!"

"Come see!"

"Never a dull moment with those two." Rising, he pulled her to her feet. "But I wouldn't have it any other way."

And neither would she.

* * * * *

If you enjoyed this story, check out these other books from author Lisa Carter:

The Deputy's Perfect Match
The Bachelor's Unexpected Family
The Christmas Baby
Hometown Reunion
His Secret Daughter
The Twin Bargain
Stranded for the Holidays

*Find these and other great reads
at www.LoveInspired.com.*

Dear Reader,

The heart of this story is about trusting God. With the good. With the bad. With everything.

After the unthinkable happened, Maggie discovered that while pain is part of the human condition, God's children don't walk the path of suffering alone. He promises to be there with them every step of the way. But instead of trusting God for the outcome, her attempts to manage her unexpected reunion only made the situation worse.

I don't know about you, but over and over again in my life, I've found myself with the exact same choice as Maggie. To trust God. Or not. To choose faith over fear. No matter what. Because that's what faith is all about—the no-matter-whats. Because of the past, Maggie believed lies about herself. But when her quest comes full circle, she learns to embrace not only the truth about her children, but about herself, too. To see herself as God sees her.

I hope that you, dear reader, fully grasp how beautiful you are to Him. A precious jewel. And so beloved. This is why I wrote this story. It is my prayer that you will walk in the truth of that realization. It's not about who you are; it is about *Whose* you are.

I hope you enjoyed taking this journey with Bridger, Maggie and the twins. I would love to hear from you. You may email me at lisa@lisacarterauthor.com or visit www.lisacarterauthor.com.

In His Love,
Lisa Carter

SPECIAL EXCERPT FROM

Sarah's long-ago love returns to her Amish community, but is he the man for her, or could her destiny lie elsewhere?

Read on for a sneak preview of
The Promise *by Patricia Davids,*
available June 2020 from HQN Books!

"Isaac is in the barn. Sarah, you should go say hello."

"Are you sure?" Sarah bit her lower lip and began walking toward the barn. Her pulse raced as butterflies filled her stomach. What would Isaac think of her? Would he be happy to see her again? What should she say? She stepped through the open doorway and paused to let her eyes adjust to the darkness. She spotted him a few feet away. He was on one knee tightening a screw in a stall door. His hat was pushed back on his head. She couldn't see his face. He hadn't heard her come in.

Suddenly she was a giddy sixteen-year-old again about to burst out laughing for the sheer joy of it. She quietly tiptoed up behind him and cupped her hands over his eyes. "Guess who?" she whispered in his ear.

"I have no idea."

The voice wasn't right. Strong hands gripped her wrists and pulled her hands away. His hat fell off as he turned his head to stare up at her. She saw a riot of dark brown curls, not straw-blond hair. She didn't know this man.

A scowl drew his brows together. "I still don't know who you are."

She pulled her hands free and stumbled backward as embarrassment robbed her of speech. The man retrieved his hat and rose to his feet. "I assume you were expecting someone else?"

"I'm sorry," she managed to squeak.

The man in front of her settled his hat on his head. He wasn't as tall as Isaac, but he was a head taller than Sarah. He had rugged good looks, dark eyes and a full mouth, which was turned up at one corner as if a grin was about to break free. "I take it you know my brother Isaac."

He was laughing at her.

The dark-haired stranger folded his arms over his chest. "I'm Levi Raber."

Of course, he would be the annoying older brother. So much for making a good first impression on Isaac's family.

Don't miss
The Promise *by Patricia Davids,*
available now wherever
HQN Books and ebooks are sold.

HQNBooks.com